Will & Patrick's Endless Honeymoon

(Wake Up Married, Episode 7)

Leta Blake

An Original Publication from Leta Blake Books
Will & Patrick's Endless Honeymoon
(Wake Up Married, Episode 7)
Written and published by Leta Blake
Cover by Dar Albert
Formatted by BB eBooks
Copyright © 2017 by Leta Blake Books
All rights reserved.

First Print Edition, 2024

Other Books by Leta Blake

Contemporary

Will & Patrick Wake Up Married
Will & Patrick's Endless Honeymoon
Cowboy Seeks Husband
The Difference Between
Bring on Forever
Stay Lucky

Sports

The River Leith

The Training Season Series
Training Season
Training Complex

Musicians

Smoky Mountain Dreams
Vespertine

New Adult

Punching the V-Card

'90s Coming of Age Series
Pictures of You
You Are Not Me
Only You

Slow Heat
Alpha Heat
Slow Birth
Bitter Heat

For Sale Series
Heat for Sale
Bully for Sale

Audiobooks
letablake.com/audiobooks

Discover more about the author online

Leta Blake
letablake.com

Gay Romance Newsletter

Leta's newsletter will keep you up to date on her latest releases, sales and deals, future writing plans, and more from the world of M/M romance. Join Leta's mailing list today.

Leta Blake on Patreon

Become part of Leta Blake's Patreon community to support her indie publishing expenses and to access exclusive content, deleted scenes, extras, and interviews.

Acknowledgements

Thank you to my patrons Sadie Sheffield, John McDonald, and all the wonderful members of my Patreon who inspire, support, and advise me. Keira Andrews for the amazing editing work. Robert Winter for his friendship and advice. And thank you to the fans of Will & Patrick who just can't get enough!

About This Book

Genius brain surgeon Patrick McCloud never thought he'd fall in love, let alone get married. He and Will Patterson are two years overdue for their honeymoon, and although romance doesn't come naturally to Patrick, he's determined to make it perfect.

Will works himself to the bone helping others and dealing with his family, who bring the drama nonstop. A tropical getaway without the usual shenanigans is just what the doctor ordered. But can Will's family leave them in peace? Knowing the Patterson-Molinaro clan, it's not likely…

Will and Patrick's Endless Honeymoon by Leta Blake continues the soapy, sexy fun of the original six part *Wake Up Married* serial. In Healing, South Dakota, marriage is never boring!

Written especially for my patrons at Patreon.com who have been supportive in every way. Dedicated to Liza who loves Will & Patrick with her whole heart.

PART ONE

Chapter One

"HOLY SMACKERONI, HOW is it still so good?" Patrick gasps, chest heaving, sweat pooling in his navel, and his groin throbbing with satisfaction.

"No idea, but I'm not complaining." Will rolls up onto his elbow to grin down at Patrick, his dark eyes alight with the afterglow. "Are you?"

"Never."

"That's what I thought." He collapses down on his back and Patrick purrs happily, rolling into his usual position with his cheek against Will's furry pecs.

After a few happy minutes of recovery time, they head into their deluxe bathroom to shower. Patrick runs his hands over Will, helping to soap him up under the streaming water. They wash away the evidence of the sex they've just had, and Patrick lingers over Will's firm buttocks and muscled abs, running his fingers over the ridges and grabbing a handful of ass.

"Been hitting the gym lately," Will whispers, as he soaps up his balls and cock, then reaches to wash off Patrick's too.

"Getting ready for our trip?"

"I want to look good for you."

"You always look good to me," Patrick says, shrugging. He thinks of the photo he keeps in his wallet from Will's days as a chubby, diabetic teen with a drinking problem. It's probably the *love* talking, but Patrick's convinced he'd have banged the hell out of sweet, sad, teen angel Will.

"And I don't understand how you always look so good," Will says, running his hands down Patrick's wiry frame and then skimming into his auburn bush and tickling against his lightly furred balls. "You eat ungodly amounts of food and yet…"

"Extra fast-twitch muscle." Patrick shrugs. His dick tingles with renewed interest. "Born with it."

"Unfair."

"If you keep playing with my balls like that, I'll end up showing you how fair I can be."

"Yeah?" Will's fingers slide back and forth over Patrick's sac. "In what way?"

"In the way where I get you off while I shoot another load up your ass."

Will's chest and cheeks are rosy from their prior round and the heat from the shower, but there's an additional flush of renewed lust. He grips Patrick's hardening cock and pumps it to full mast. "Show me."

Patrick reaches for the small jar of coconut oil they keep by the shampoo for this very reason. Will's still relaxed from their romp on the bed, and, after coating his own dick with oil, it's easy enough for Patrick to flip

Will around to the wall, spread his cheeks apart, and press into his tight asshole.

Will moans and pushes back, bearing down as Patrick slides right in. It's a glorious sight. It always is. Seeing his dick disappear into Will, seeing Will's back flush with effort, watching the gooseflesh break over Will's skin, and hearing his sweet, urgent sounds. Always ready. Always eager.

Will is such a beautiful fuck.

Patrick grips Will's wet shoulders and sets up a strong rhythm. The water rushes down Patrick's back and ass, a warm, wet compliment to the tight clutch of Will's body around his cock. He rests his forehead on Will's upper back and fucks him hard. The slap of their bodies echoes around their bathroom, the wetness adding a bit of sting to each sharp thrust.

He's not a kid anymore and he came once already, but it's not long before he feels the building pleasure, the tension and rush of semen, and he reaches around to make sure he fulfills his promise of getting Will off first.

Will's hard cock leaks slick precome as Patrick pounds his prostate, and he shudders hard against Patrick's body when Patrick takes him roughly in hand. "Let's see you paint the tiles," Patrick whispers and jerks him hard and fast, making Will squirm and back up onto Patrick's cock.

"Yeah," Will whimpers, as Patrick works him. "That's...oh!" He freezes and pushes his ass back, taking Patrick's plunging dick with his wide-open, hungry hole, and then he convulses hard, his ass tightening ruthlessly on Patrick and his cock going hotter and harder in Patrick's relentless hand.

"Oh!" Will shouts again, his hands scrambling for purchase on the wet tiles. His shoulders jump tightly as his cock pumps streaks of white come over the bathroom tiles, and his ass works around Patrick's aching cock.

"Good job," Patrick mutters, reaching down to cup Will's balls as he thrusts deep and grips Will's hip with the other hand. "Good…job…" he grunts out again and throws his head back, staring at the white ceiling as pleasure grips him and he shoots up into Will in hard, sweet jolts.

Groaning and coming down from the sharp high of orgasm, he feels raw and tender all over, and his cock is sensitive encased in Will's still-trembling body. He kisses Will's shoulder blades and the visible knobs of his spine, before rubbing his face against the hair at the nape of Will's neck.

"Careful," Will whispers as Patrick eases out of him. They're both shaky and unsteady on their feet. "Don't fall."

Patrick laughs under his breath as he reaches for the slick wall to hold himself up. "Puddin'-pop, that sweet butt of yours sucked out my strength."

"No, just your soul." Will turns to help hold Patrick up, even though he's shaking too.

"I'd agree if I believed in souls."

"But you believe in astrology."

"Astrology is—"

"Shh. Let's get clean now." Will yawns widely, his pearly whites gleaming in the light bouncing off the walls. He splashes water on the strings of come clinging to the tiles and Patrick's inexplicably sad to see it washed away.

"Distraction. That's a Libra move."

"Mmm-hmm, I know." Will grabs more soap and starts on his ass, biting his lower lip as he washes his hole.

"Leave some of me up in you," Patrick says, his voice rough. "I like knowing my boys are in your colon looking desperately for an egg to knock up."

Will laughs and pulls Patrick back beneath the shower stream again. "Let me help you." The water stays warm and steady as Will soaps Patrick's cock again, leaving them both loose-limbed and utterly sated by the time Will turns the shower off and reaches for a towel.

Back in the bedroom, Patrick grabs Will's insulin pump from the bedside table, uncaps the infusion site cap, and reattaches the lines. "Test," he says, handing Will the kit. "Make sure you don't need an additional bolus."

Will rolls his eyes but gamely pricks his finger and shrugs at the results. "All good."

Patrick grabs the monitor to check for himself. Nodding at the readings, he hands the monitor back to Will, climbs into bed, and tugs Will into their favorite position. Then he nestles against his favorite furry pillow again and closes his eyes, ready to drift off to sleep for a few hours before he'll need to be up early for surgery.

He's beyond content. He's what he'd call happy even. He and Will are just over two years into this life together, but happiness is still a reasonably new emotion for him. So he wallows in it aggressively every chance he gets, indulging in moony feelings for Will and feeling *grateful*, of all things. He's glad no one else can hear his gross, ooey-gooey thoughts.

"I love you," Will whispers.

Patrick's heart clenches with joy and he nuzzles his face against Will's chest hair. "Good."

"Just 'good'? You don't want to, I don't know, reciprocate the declaration?"

"You already know how I feel." Patrick huffs. "I married you, didn't I? Twice. Just to prove I meant it the first time."

Will laughs.

The sound is intimate in their warm, soft cocoon of a bed, lit only by the yellow light from the nightstands. Patrick's not an overly sentimental man, but he reaches out to finger the medical ID bracelet on Will's wrist, the one he'd gotten him that first Christmas, and smiles softly. "Fine. I love you," he whispers. "Even if you should already know."

"Oh, I know."

Will kisses the top of Patrick's head and it's sweet and perfect. Their warm, naked bodies tangle together, and all they need to do is turn off the lights and drift away.

So, of course his phone picks this moment to start vibrating. And worse, playing a very specific ringtone—Drake's "Bitch Is Crazy."

Will groans. "I thought I told you to change that."

"And I ignored you."

Will grabs his own phone from the nightstand, habitually set to silent after nine at night to try to avoid family drama. Too bad the *entire* Patterson-Molinaro clan has Patrick's phone number now. None of them are afraid to use it. And Patrick's a neurosurgeon, so he can't turn his off on a whim like Will can.

Will groans. "Three missed calls from her. It's almost midnight. What could she want?"

Patrick rolls away from Will before passing his vibrating, Drake-playing iPhone over to him. "You answer. She's your mother."

Will heaves up to sitting and tugs the blankets to cover his nakedness like Kimberly is going to somehow *see* him all flushed and satisfied.

"Mom, it's late."

Patrick can hear Kimberly's voice clear as a bell from his side of the bed. Either she's talking loudly or he needs to turn the volume down on his phone. Regardless, she's annoying. He already misses the perfection of just a few seconds ago.

"William Patterson, don't take that tone with me. This is an emergency!"

Will's breath quickens and he sits up even straighter. "Is it Connor? Olivia? Are you at the hospital?"

"It's Caitlin," she moans.

"What's happened?" Will starts to stand, but Patrick jerks him back down to the bed, shaking his head. "Do I need to come?"

Now that she's roped Will in, Kimberly drops her faux-angst down to mere soap-opera levels. "She's leaving for college tomorrow. *Tomorrow!* What will I do without her?"

Will rubs his eyes. "Mom, we can talk about this over coffee in the morning at Brown Gargle. I'll meet you at eight-thirty, all right?"

"No, it is *not* all right, Will!"

Patrick really hates Kimberly sometimes. She always knows how to get Will wound up. He taps his fingers against the cover and listens as Will does his thing and tries to calm her down.

"I know it's hard to let go of us kids. But it's part of the circle of—"

"It complicates everything, baby. Who's going to watch Connor after school? Who's going to take Olivia to her piano lessons?"

Patrick rolls his eyes.

Will takes a long, slow breath in, obviously gathering his patience. "Olivia hates piano, Mom. Let her quit."

"Olivia needs to learn how to play an instrument."

"Why?"

"Because she lacks any discipline in her life."

"Wait, what?" Will's nostrils flare. "*You're* talking about discipline?"

"Yes, I am!" Kimberly's on fire now. Patrick's never going to get to sleep. "And why shouldn't she learn? Patrick plays piano and look where he is in life. *He's* a neurosurgeon."

Patrick rolls his eyes. Again. About time he finally gets some credit from his mother-in-law for being a whiz-bang, mega-awesome, crack-open-the-skull doctor for cripes sake, but this conversation still needs to be nipped in the bud.

He nudges Will's leg and shakes his head. "Off topic."

Will sighs and tries a firmer voice. "Mom, we can and will solve these problems, okay? Together. But not right now. Patrick has early surgery in the morning and you woke us up."

Patrick snorts as Kimberly wails. "Will, how am I supposed to get any rest tonight when I'm not sure how I'll manage—"

Patrick grabs the phone from Will's hand. "Goodnight, Kimberly. Don't call back. Your inane crisis can wait." He disconnects the call and quickly blocks her number. He'll unblock her again in the morning and they can endure her wrath then.

Endure, ignore. Same difference.

There are many days he wishes he could be done with Kimberly Patterson forever, but, for better or worse, Will and his family are a package deal.

"There. Handled." Patrick tosses his phone back on the nightstand. "Bedtime now."

Will's lips work and Patrick thinks he's about to be told off for being an asshole. Instead, Will bursts into laughter. "Seriously, she's impossible."

"If only. Alas, she's entirely possible. Proof is rendered daily."

Will groans. "I can't wait for our honeymoon trip next week. We've put it off too long. I love my family—I do—but it'll be good to get away from them. Very far away, hopefully."

"We could get away from them forever if you just say the word." Patrick ignores the subtle dig for info on their trip and guides Will back down in the bed. "I'm tired. Be the pillow."

Will opens his arms and Patrick snuggles in close. "You'd never leave Healing, Patrick. You love your unit and Jenny and Dylan. And my family."

"I love the kids. Your mother? Not so much." Patrick kisses Will's chest and closes his eyes. "Now go to sleep."

Will flips out the light on the nightstand and strokes Patrick's shoulder lightly. The glug-glug of Will's steady heartbeat and the susurration of his breath lull Patrick into dreams.

And before he knows it, the alarm is going off and he hits the ground running for another day as Healing, South Dakota's superhero neurosurgeon, while his sexy sidekick dresses for his day of dynamic do-gooding.

Their lives are hectic, but, in Patrick's estimation, great. He wouldn't change a thing. Much.

Chapter Two

D ESPITE THE FANTASTIC before-sleep sex, a full six hours of rest, and the general pleasantness of his usual morning routine with Patrick, Will walks into Brown Gargle with a headache growing behind his eyes.

His usually comfortable button-up blue shirt feels itchy, and his new leather loafers are a pinch too tight. His chest is tight too.

Despite plenty of interactions over the last few years, Will knows his mom has never really grown accustomed to Patrick's gruff side. And, despite explaining to her that Patrick is on the autism spectrum and doesn't always understand the nuances of social interactions, she doesn't seem to get it. Always declaring that 'excuses like that' only go so far.

Never mind that his mom's own behavior leaves a lot to be desired socially, in Will's opinion. But she'll never see herself the way he does, and Will can't begin to explain it to her without another relationship tsunami rising between them. So he just has to grin and bear it. Again.

He smooths his hands through his hair and takes a

calming breath.

Whatever she has to say to him, it'll be fine. Patrick will be waiting for him this evening at home and, no matter what level of crazy his mother brings, they will be *fine*.

He just wishes his headache agreed with him.

Will checks his monitor and gets a good BG reading. So it's probably not a glucose spike and his pump is most likely working fine. It's just stress and that won't end until he's out of his mother's clutches for the day.

Jax Taken Alive is behind the counter looking a bit tired and grim. His dark hair is growing out in a hip, rock-star-esque shag these days, but there's a tension to his expression that isn't usually there. The morning doesn't seem to be agreeing with him either. That or he and Jenny are arguing again.

"Hey, man," Will says, pulling out his wallet to pay for the Buckaroo-sized coffee that Jax is already pouring. "Can I get a jelly donut too?"

"Sure. Patrick coming or are you alone?" Jax asks, indicating the cups he uses to make Patrick's usual Calamalatte Jane.

"Just me." Will smiles and stuffs a five in the tip jar. "You okay? You look—" he waves a hand over his own face and says nothing.

"The usual." Jax shrugs, getting the jelly donut from the display case and shoving it into a small takeout bag without asking Will if he's staying or going. "She'll either get over the age difference or she won't."

"Yeah," Will agrees, taking the bag and the to-go cup without protest. "It's not like you can do anything about it."

And it's been over *two years*. Will doesn't understand why Jenny won't just move on from either the problem or from Jax. One way or the other, she needs to choose. It's cruel to keep torturing Jax this way.

Jax leans forward. "I'm aiming to do something about it."

"Oh, yeah? What's that?"

"I haven't told many people, so keep this to yourself, but I'm working out a deal with Old Man Hart to buy him out of this place."

"Wow, so he's looking to leave the business?"

"He wants to retire to Cali to be near his grandkids. But I want to convince Jenny to marry me. Buying him out seems like a good first step toward showing her I'm not a kid."

"You're older than me. What makes her think you're a kid?"

Jax raises a dark brow. "You run a massive charitable foundation. I'm a barista."

"You aren't just a barista. You manage this place. Old Man Hart's never here. You keep it going."

He shrugs. "In Jenny's eyes, I'm still the kid barista she somehow fell into screwing and can't seem to stop. She won't even tell me she loves me."

"What?" That seems absurd. Jenny was instrumental in getting Patrick to accept and declare his feelings for

Will, and she'd wanted to beat up Will when he'd failed to declare his own in a way that prevented Patrick's heart from being temporarily broken.

Now it turns out she's a withholding jerk about her own heart? Will wonders what Patrick has to say about *that*.

Jax shrugs. "Baggage. From Tom."

"The only thing Tom was good for was making Dylan," Will says, sipping his coffee, and glancing around to see if his mom is already somewhere in the shop waiting impatiently to needle him with guilt. "Jenny's better off without that guy in every other way. It's good that he left."

Jax's dark eyebrows draw lower. "He's been calling her again."

"No way."

"Wants to see Dylan."

"Wow." Dylan is three now, and Tom hasn't been interested before. "What's she going to do?"

The bell rings on the door behind him and Jax steps back from the counter when he sees who it is. "You'll have to ask Jenny. Meantime, I think your coffee date is here. I'll get her Americano West prepared and bring it on over."

"William Patterson." His mother's voice is scolding and full of pain all at once.

Will sighs and turns around, his head throbbing again. "Mom. Hey, did you sleep okay?"

"I most certainly did not." She turns up her pretty

nose and sniffs. The purple silk of her clingy summer dress shows off her cleavage and hips nicely. Her makeup is flatteringly done, and her long blond hair flips under at the ends. The cowboy boots are the only giveaway that she works every day at a tack shop and is an excellent horsewoman.

"I'm sorry you didn't sleep well. I thought I did, but I guess not, since I've got a rotten headache this morning."

"Have you checked your BG?" she asks, her eyes widening in concern.

"Of course. It's fine. I'm fine." He smiles and takes hold of her elbow. "C'mon. Let's find a seat. Jax saw you come in and he'll have your usual right over."

"And I'd like a Honeybear Bar too," she calls over her shoulder as Will steers her toward a private table near the front.

"Yes, ma'am," Jax answers with a nod, but without the handsome, flirty grin he usually shoots at pretty customers.

Will makes a mental note to follow up with him about Jenny later or poke at Patrick to see what he knows. The fact that Tom is back in the picture is a complication Jax doesn't need. Will feels for the guy, but Jenny is Patrick's best friend, and if things ever truly fall apart, he knows which side he'll have to take to keep the peace in his own life.

Not that Patrick won't tell Jenny all the ways she's being an asshole if he doesn't think she's being fair. But, in the end, Patrick and Jenny are a forever thing, even if Jax and Jenny aren't. Will knows it. Jax knows it. The whole world knows it. Heck, even Kimberly probably knows it.

Speaking of, his mother is busy powdering her nose and looking offended. He'll have to break the ice.

"So, you're worried about Caitlin going off to college, huh?" He's going to stop by the house after work so he can say goodbye to his sister and make sure Caitlin knows he's there for her anytime for anything.

"You didn't think it was important last night, why do you want to talk about it now?" She blinks at him angrily, which is a thing he's never known a person can do until now.

Stalling, he takes a bite of jelly donut and chews slowly.

She eyes him for a long moment and then finally says, "It's still unnerving to watch you eat without giving yourself a shot first."

Will smiles and wipes his fingers on a napkin. "For me too, but it's been a good switch."

Sometimes he wishes he'd kept on giving himself insulin injections despite Patrick's urging to try out the newest sensor and pump advertised as the world's first "artificial pancreas." Even though there haven't been any malfunctions, Will can't stop the occasional paranoia, especially after semi-rough sex or going out riding, that the sensor may have dislodged and his monitor might not be getting the right readings to dispense insulin.

But Patrick is fastidious about checking the sensor and infusion sites, morning and night, and there's never been an incident. So Will continues on with the pump. It's freeing in a lot of ways—he can travel more easily and eat without the whole test, calc, stick routine. More importantly, he's gone nine months without an A1C higher than six, which means better overall health in the long run.

Patrick loves that he can check the readings on his phone and gets alerts to any big dip or rise in Will's blood sugar. Still, Will misses the sense of control shots always afforded him and the comfort of knowing exactly how much insulin is going into his body at any point in time.

He tries again. "About Caitlin."

"What about her?"

"Mom."

Kimberly tucks her hair behind her ears and snarls, "He said I was inane."

She isn't using Patrick's name, so that mean's she's still angry. At least she isn't calling him 'that doctor' or 'that man' the way she did when they were first married.

"No, Patrick said your *crisis* was inane."

She narrows her eyes. "You always defend him. I'm your mother. You could defend me for once."

"It was late. He was tired and he had an important surgery early this morning." One Patrick's been anxious to have behind him so he can go on their honeymoon trip with a clear conscience. "Honestly, the conversation could wait. It *did* wait. The world hasn't ended yet."

She lifts one carefully sculpted brow. "More defense of his behavior and more patronizing of me and my concerns."

Guilt slithers through Will's gut. Has he dismissed her unfairly? Caitlin *is* going very far away, and while the two of them have been on precarious terms for years now, Kimberly will certainly be feeling the pangs any mother does when her offspring grows up and leaves the nest.

Jax drops off Kimberly's order and she presses a twenty into his hand. "Keep the change, sweetheart," she says with a smile that raises the hackles on the back of Will's neck.

"He's Jenny Burger's boyfriend," Will says warningly when Jax walks away.

"He's not her husband."

Will takes a deep breath. Jax is a big boy and can fend off any advances Kimberly makes. Probably. It's just annoying to see his mother already turning to her usual way of dealing with emotions she doesn't want to feel: beginning an inappropriate love affair with whatever handsome man catches her eye.

"Mom, I have to get to work before long. Can we please talk about Caitlin now?"

Kimberly's eyes leave Jax's tight ass and focus on Will again. "Why couldn't she have gone to the University of South Dakota like you did? Vermillion is too far away to be of much use to me, but at least she could have come home quickly enough if there was an emergency."

"Because she's had her heart set on the fashion merchandising program at Colorado State for the last year and a half. That's what she's been working for, why she broke things off with Scott Tate and got so focused in school. She's figured out what she wants, and she's not going to let anything get in the way of having it. You should be proud of her. I am."

"She never could have gone if you hadn't paid for it," Kimberly says somewhat accusingly.

"Like Nonna wouldn't have paid if I hadn't?" Caitlin isn't his Nonna's granddaughter by blood, but she loves her just the same.

"Because she's your sister and Eleanora knows you adore Caitlin."

For a lot of years, 'adore' might have been overstating it. Caitlin was a pill throughout her puberty and adolescence, but she's coming out the other side now. In fact, sometimes Will can see the woman she's going to be and that vision makes his heart sing.

"You've always been her favorite grandchild. She ignores all her others."

Will sighs. Clearly he's not going to win with his mother today. Not at anything. So he eats more of his donut and sips his coffee, grateful that his headache seems to be diminishing. Sometimes the anticipation of interacting with his mother is worse than the real thing. And sometimes it's not.

Kimberly sips her coffee and then says primly, "I didn't appreciate Patrick dismissing me so callously last night."

"He's Patrick, Mom."

"He's an intelligent man who can be charming when he wants to be—*obviously* since he's managed to win you over heart and soul—but he never bothers extending that charm to me."

Charming isn't quite the right word for Patrick *ever*, but Will doesn't see the point of arguing it. People who like Patrick—and people Patrick likes back—are fine with him the way he is, the way he *always* is, because Patrick doesn't change. It's one of Will's favorite things about him.

"We've had this conversation before and it never goes well." Will smiles tensely. "Can we focus on Caitlin? You seemed to think her leaving constituted a national crisis last night."

"Be a smart mouth if you want, but it is a *real* crisis, Will. Especially with you and Patrick leaving soon for your ridiculously self-indulgent holiday."

"You realize you're talking about our honeymoon?"

"It's not a honeymoon, baby," she says with a frosty dollop of condescending scolding. "You've been married for well over two years." She sips her coffee and rolls her eyes.

"Exactly. We've put it off long enough."

Kimberly slips her fingers through her blond hair. "This honeymoon doesn't help your sister get to her soccer games or piano lessons, and it doesn't help Connor get from school out to the farm, and it doesn't help me with—"

"Mom, I get it. You're put out by me and Caitlin not being at your beck and call." He reaches out to take her hand, squeezing her cool fingers gently. "But I believe in you. You can do this without us."

She jerks her hand back. "Don't be condescending to your mother."

Will ignores that and goes on calmly, "Besides, Patrick and I will only be gone ten days. When we get back, we'll host the kids for a week."

He frowns. Why did he offer to do that? He isn't doing anything wrong by taking a honeymoon with his husband, and yet his mother makes him feel like he hasn't earned it, and, worse, needs to make up for it. Not that Patrick will mind Olivia and Connor staying at the house for a while, but he'll definitely have something to say about how Will came to agree to the whole thing.

He sighs. Can he ever escape his instinctive reactions to his mother's machinations?

"That will be helpful." Kimberly brightens a bit. "In the meantime, though, I'm not quite sure what I should do with them. Someone has to run the tack store. Since Jason quit, I haven't had any good help."

Will clenches his jaw. Jason Kirkpatrick had been his mother's last on-and-off boyfriend. He'd finally decided to be done with Kimberly for good after Tony Molinaro, Will's father, breezed through town to tumble Kimberly in numerous and various ways, and in way-too-public places.

When Jason got word that Kimberly had cheated for the third—fourth?—time, he quit both his job as the manager of the tack shop and the town altogether, moving to Idaho to take a ranch hand position.

Will never liked Jason that much, but he hates what his mother does to men. "There were good reasons he quit, you realize."

She waves him off. "I'm in no mood for one of your lectures about addiction and your father and me."

"It's not like I don't know about addiction, Mom."

"And how is that going? How many months sober now?"

Will flinches. She knows it's been since the night he and Patrick got married (the first time). He's not going to indulge her waspish question with an answer. "Anyway, about the tack shop. I'm sure you could find some good help if you advertised on the rez."

She shrugs and sips her coffee again. "Perhaps. That won't solve my problems entirely, not when Caitlin is gone and you're in…" Her eyes glint curiously. "Where is it you're going on this honeymoon?"

"It's a secret."

"Right. A secret from your own mother."

It's a secret from *him* actually. Patrick's planned the whole thing, probably with Jenny's help, and Will doesn't know their destination. He hopes it's somewhere warm, but, otherwise, he's excited to see what Patrick's idea of a honeymoon looks like.

"Mom, we'll be gone ten days. You'll manage. Reba will help you and I'm sure you can get Kevin to do a bit more. I know he got a housekeeper after Grandma Betty…" he trails off.

He doesn't like to mention his grandmother's death to Kimberly. It sets off a whole other string of woe about how she's been left alone, an orphan in the world, with only her brother and four ungrateful children to care for her now.

"You make it sound so easy, but you have no idea how Caitlin's leaving is going to disrupt the fabric of our lives."

"And you've known she's going to Colorado for how long? You've had plenty of time to make arrangements. Hire a nanny. If the expense is too much, then I'll help out. It's not a problem."

"A nanny! You're willing to fob off your siblings on a stranger?"

Will rubs his face and his phone vibrates in his pocket. He glances down to see that his BG is going high and that his pump is dispensing extra insulin.

"Who's texting?" Kimberly asks.

"It's nothing. No one." He slides the phone back in his pocket. "We live in Healing, Mom. There are no strangers here. Hire a nanny. Just for a few months. If we don't like her, we'll let her go."

She glares at him a long moment. "We'd need to have a thorough background check done and—"

Will smiles. "I'll put Nonna on it. You'll have some-one before Patrick and I leave town. I promise."

Kimberly relaxes like a child who's finally gotten her way and eats her donut happily.

Crisis averted.

Will doesn't feel like eating more and simply sips his coffee, chatting with her about the recent delivery of two new horses at the farm. He knows Kevin's working on breaking the stallion.

"What are your plans for the rest of the day?" Will asks.

"I need to get to the store," his mother says, glancing at her phone. "And then I have to go out to the farm to consult with Kevin about those new horses. What's on your agenda?"

"Good Works this morning and then I have an ap-pointment." He doesn't say it's with Caitlin at the house, because he knows their mother will "drop by" to join them if he does.

"Well, don't forget to make time to say goodbye to your sister. She sounds like she never intends to come home." Kimberly's eyes grow wet but she stands up with a determined expression, kissing Will's cheek. "Have a good day, baby. Give Patrick my love."

Will watches her go, confused as always by her about-face on Patrick, and gathers his things. Waving to Jax, he heads out into the warm late-August morning.

Chapter Three

"DO YOU HAVE rocks for brains?" Patrick snaps, rubbing the ache at his temples.

The other nurse at the station tenses up, but the one he's talking to just raises a brow.

"Do *you* have an attorney at the ready to handle the harassment case I'll slap on you if you keep talking to me like that?" Varun Choudry crosses his arms over the front of his scrubs. "They don't pay me enough to deal with you."

"That's the truth." And despite Patrick's best efforts, he hasn't managed to fix that problem yet. He looks at the computer again, scanning the patient's chart. "I know you're not stupid, but you—"

"Careful," Varun purrs. "That almost sounds like flirting."

"Ha! As if."

He's come to know Varun well since the night the young, handsome nurse hit on him in the bar of the Tallgrass hotel. Luckily, Will likes him too, and once tried to set Varun up with an employee of Good Works, but Varun wasn't interested.

Varun keeps his brow arched. "Look, I told you. When I came in, five hundred milligrams of Keppra was charted. I can't give her more if it's on the chart. And it's *on the chart.*"

"But it's not *in her body.* This chart is a lie!"

Varun sighs. "Then order more and I'll give it to her, but I can't give her more on my own authority if it's charted that she's received her dose. You know this."

"And you *know* she didn't receive it."

Varun scowls at him.

Patrick scowls back. "Fine. Give a STAT one-time dose of oral five hundred milligrams Keppra. And grab some urine beforehand and send it to the labs to test. I want to confirm what I already know. Then you can chart it all."

"Will do." Varun bats his pretty eyes. "Enter the order and we're a go, Dr. McFlirty."

The brunette ponytailed nurse who's clacking away on the other computer gasps slightly and turns red. Patrick can just imagine all the ways she'll misrepresent this interaction with Varun to the hospital administration given half the chance.

Patrick's one of the only doctors who has the nurses' backs when salary disputes come up in the boardroom, but they don't know that. So this one's probably planning to gab to anyone upstairs who will listen about his supposedly inappropriate behavior with a coworker.

"Oh, can it," he says to her irritably, holding up his left hand. "I'm a married man. Go be a stick-in-the-mud in room 8-B. She needs her bedpan changed."

"Yes, Dr. McCloud." The nurse hustles off, her cheeks still stained red.

"Don't be a jerk to Lizzy."

"I'll be a jerk to whomever I want."

"Enter the order, Dr. McCloud," Varun says again, rolling his eyes. "I thought there was no time to waste."

"I'm a brain surgeon not a babysitter. You enter the order."

Varun cocks his hip. "As you well know, new hospital policy says *you* have to enter the order, not me."

"Fine." Patrick grumbles under his breath about ridiculous new hospital policies that just waste his time and jerk nurses who're going to get him written up for sexual harassment, when all he wants to do is saw into someone's head and fix their brains. "When you're fired for being a pain in my butt, don't come whining to me."

"I'm shaking in my boots." Varun laughs.

"You should be."

"Why would you get me fired when you're always trying to convince me to come aboard full time and give up my travel contract?"

Patrick punches the buttons on the keyboard. "You've been here for years. Give up the ruse that you're still a travel nurse."

"Not until the hospital gives a livable salary. Once they stop paying their staff nurses less than those on travel contracts, I'll give it some thought."

Patrick frowns. He's still angry he lost that argument

in the last board meeting. It makes no sense not to make it worth it to good nurses to come on full time.

It's not like Healing has anything else to offer them. Crummy weather nine months of the year, almost-decent schooling for their kids, and becoming the subject of vicious, small town gossip are about it. If Healing Regional wants to make a name for itself, if it really wants to become a first class medical facility, then they need to cough up livable full-time salaries plus great benefits.

Varun deserves to get paid enough to make a home here. But maybe he hasn't found a real reason to stay yet, since he hasn't found a doctor to marry him. That's his self-proclaimed goal in life, and Patrick's made zero headway in getting him to understand that it's a dumb one.

"What is it about STAT you don't understand?" he barks, finishing up the order and stepping away from the computer.

Varun smiles warmly at him. "Good job, Dr. McCloud. I'll get right on that."

Patrick snorts as Varun leaves. "Hey!" Patrick calls out to him. "Text me the name of the nurse who charted that dose."

Varun walks backward as he answers, "You talked with her and gave her the order personally, plus her name was on the chart too. I thought you were a genius. Don't you remember?"

"I don't bother remembering the names of people

who're going to be fired by the end of the day." She had blond hair, though. He remembers that.

Varun sighs. "I won't text it. But I'll give you a hint. Ruby Lovell."

"What's that?"

"Her name, genius."

Then Varun disappears around the corner, and Patrick sets out toward Don Knife's office to make a giant stinking fuss about nurses who chart things they don't actually do.

But before he makes it there, he's waylaid by the sight of one of only a handful of people he cares enough about to stop and talk to. "Jenny, what are you doing here?"

She's parked in a chair outside one of the labs. Her wide smile is as blinding as ever, brightening the fluorescent hospital hallway. "Follow-up from that raging UTI I had last month. Now that I'm down a kidney, they want to make sure everything is cleared up."

He takes the empty seat beside her as a tall nurse squeaks past them both in her rubber-soled shoes. "Where's Dylan?"

Jenny tightens her glossy, blond ponytail. "At that new Mother's Day Out program the Methodist church is hosting." Her blue eyes grow damp. "Can you believe he's old enough to go to one of those now?"

"Hmmph." He *can* believe it actually. Dylan isn't the sweet, drooling six-month-old he first met anymore. He's a tyrant of a three-year-old, and Jenny's got her hands full. He's still a cute little booger.

"Why so grumpy?" she asks, twisting in her seat and stuffing her phone into her mammoth purse.

"Who says I'm grumpy?"

"C'mon. Tell me."

"Doctor stuff. Confidential. Yadda."

Jenny rolls her eyes. "Oh, well, if that's all it is, go on your way. I'd just gotten to the good part in the ridiculous vampire romance I'm reading." She fishes her phone back out of her purse and opens the reading app.

Patrick almost asks for the title, he needs a trashy read for his upcoming trip, but he says, "I have to go on a honeymoon. For ten days. *Ten.*"

"Aha!" Jenny pokes him in the arm and stuffs her phone back in her purse. "I knew you were going to freak out about that sooner or later."

"How am I supposed to do nothing for ten days?"

"We've made a great plan, Patrick. There's plenty of stuff to do at the resorts. And, if you don't want to do those things after all, you can read. Nap. Have sex. Walk on the beach. Meditate. Take up smoking weed." She ticks these off on her fingers.

Patrick huffs. "Patients need me. I can't go gallivanting—"

"It's your honeymoon."

"What was Will thinking to ask me—"

"He's thinking that he loves you and wants to be alone with you in a romantic location for an extended period of time." She takes hold of his hand and twines their fingers together. "No patients. No family. No drama."

No family and no drama. Jenny is selling it hard now, speaking right to his heart.

She smiles. "And there *are* other good neurosurgeons on staff—"

"Not half as good as me."

"Maybe not. But you approved their hire so they must be competent enough to care for your patients for ten days." She squeezes his hand, tilting her head earnestly. "I've had a pep talk ready to go for a few weeks now. Do you want to hear it?"

"Why do you think I brought this up?"

"Right. Okay." She takes a deep breath, smiles at another nurse who trundles past with an empty patient bed, then gives him her "this is serious" face. "Patrick McCloud, you will go on this honeymoon and you will love it. Do you understand me? Will deserves this. He's been through hell, deals with his crazy family, and, and, *and!* He's never been anywhere, despite having more money than God, because he's never felt allowed to go. Don't be another person who holds him back. He's your true love, your sweet, patient puddin'-pop, and he wants this so much. He's been hinting at it for years before he flat out asked you if you'd be willing. You know it'll make him happy, right?"

"Yes."

"And making him happy is your number one goal in life?"

Patrick rubs his nose. "It is."

She nods. "Exactly. Case closed. You'll go and have fun. No more panicking."

"What if something goes wrong while I'm gone?"

"Like with Addison?"

Patrick's lips tighten. He's lost other patients since fifteen-year-old Addison died while he was in surgery with another patient, but she still weighs on his mind. Especially lately. Maybe it's because Caitlin is going to college and it reminds him that Addison should have been on her way too. Or maybe it's because this is a small town, and every year people put flowers by the tree Addison's parents planted in her memory. He can't ever forget.

"You're not a god," Jenny whispers as a pair of doctors Patrick vaguely recognizes as being from obstetrics stroll past. "There are no guarantees, whether it's you or some other doctor."

Patrick rolls his eyes. Those are his own words being parroted back at him. He says them often enough when outcomes aren't as rosy as he'd hoped.

"What else is bugging you?" Jenny prods. "Get it out now, so you don't take it home and spill it all over Will."

"I don't *do* vacations." He prefers his days structured. He likes to get up, work, eat, watch some TV, screw Will, sleep, and then work some more. If he has to fit in some time with Will's family somewhere in there, or take a phone call from Dinah, then so be it. The rest of the structure gives him a sense of safety and control. It gives him something to *do* in the world; it tells him how to *be*.

"All the more reason to take one, then."

"Easy for you to say."

"You and I made a long list of potential activities. Plus there's always sex. You love that. It's a fun way to fill a day." She grins.

"Yes, but Will's asshole can only take so much screwing." Though he has a plan for that. The truth is, he's just panicking because the trip is looming near. He knows, deep down, he'll be fine. This is just the last-minute tantrum he has to throw to accept the inevitability of it all.

Jenny sighs. "Here you are whining about going on an amazing honeymoon when I haven't been on a real vacation in forever. Maybe *I* should go with Will instead of you."

"That would definitely undermine any hope of achieving my number one goal in life."

Jenny laughs. "True. I guess I have to stay here with Dylan and my…" Her brow furrows. "I was going to say my man, but I think I broke up with him again last night."

Patrick catches her eye. "You think? Or you did?"

"I did." She wrinkles her nose and gives him her patented innocent expression.

Patrick huffs. "Finally. Good riddance."

Jenny rolls her eyes. "Reverse psychology won't work with me, buster."

"No reverse psychology here. This is all going to

plan." Patrick smirks.

"Meaning?"

"The man's a dreamboat. Now that you're done with him, he can join me and Will as a third in our bed."

"Ha! As if you'd share Will!"

Patrick shrugs, but she's right. He and Will are way too absorbed in each other to want to be with anyone else. "So what happened this time? The D finally stopped being so good?"

Her smile is wicked. "No, the D has always been consistently slamming. Hello, raging UTI, remember?" She goes wistful obviously remembering Jax and his D, but then rubs at her forehead. "I guess that's over."

Patrick nudges her. "So he stopped being handsome and funny?"

Her blue eyes cut into him. "Stop being a jerk. You know what the problem is!"

"I do. You're a snob."

She sits up straighter. "I am not."

"You are. You're a regular old-fashioned snob and you think you're too good for him."

"That's bullshit."

"Is it really just the barista thing or is it racism too? It's because he's Lakota, right?"

"Don't be a bastard today, Patrick. I don't feel up to listening to it. And after I just gave you a great pep talk."

"It sucks when I'm right. Oh, wait, I'm always right."

She glares. "It's not that he's Lakota. I don't care about that. It's his lack of ambition."

"As evidenced by…?"

She counts the reasons on her fingers. "He doesn't have a college education. He doesn't want to ever leave Healing. He plans to work in that coffee shop indefinitely."

"*Manage* that coffee shop," Patrick corrects.

"It's a coffee shop, Patrick."

"Like I said, you're a snob."

"Oh, and you aren't a snob?" She flips her ponytail pointedly. "Like you'd have found Will half as attractive without his money and career?"

"Will's a desperate do-gooder." Patrick shrugs. "He wears the look well. But, yes, I'd have loved him without the money."

"You only say that because you're head-over-heels for him now. But if you're being honest…" She leans forward and narrows her eyes. "The money was *literally* the only reason you didn't divorce him immediately."

Patrick raises his brows. "Well, if you want to be *literal* about it—something you and Will tell me *not* to be, by the way—that's true."

"It is true!" She jabs a pink-painted fingernail into his arm. "You only came to Healing because you didn't want him to lose all that mobster-funded Molinaro trust money."

"No, I came because *he* didn't want to lose the money."

"God, you're so literal!" she exclaims.

"You just told me to be."

The money that funds Will's charitable foundation, Good Works, does a lot of good things in the world, despite its blood money origins. Will's foundation provides help to kids with cancer and supports LGBT kids in rural areas, amongst many other amazing and ridiculously do-gooder-y things.

Patrick concedes, "Fine. I have a soft spot for kids with cancer."

"And a soft spot for Will."

"Sue me."

"It's just you don't understand what it's like for me."

Patrick says nothing. He can't dispute that. He can try to be a good friend, but Jenny is always a little bit of a mystery to him. Most people are.

She sits stiffly for a long second, then turns to him, grips his forearm, and confesses, "I don't know what to do. Tom's been calling me. He wants to see Dylan. He claims to want to work it out. As a family. A real family."

Patrick rolls his eyes before throwing his arm around Jenny's shoulder and pulling her in close to whisper in her ear, "He walked out on you when you were pregnant. Get real."

"I am real," she protests, pulling away. "I'm a real woman with real feelings and I *really* don't know what I should do."

Patrick opens his mouth and closes it again. He should say something helpful, but he has no idea what that might be.

"I think I have to give it a shot."

"You don't have to do anything."

"Okay, then, I want to. I want to see what Tom might bring to the table. For Dylan. And for me."

"What's his sign?"

Jenny smirks. "Pisces."

"Hmm. Well, all right then." At least the guy isn't a Sagittarius.

"Glad I have your permission," she whispers.

At that moment, Patrick spots Kimberly and her twin brother Kevin walking arm-in-arm through the hospital corridor.

Kevin's wearing a nice-fitting pair of jeans and a plaid, Western-wear shirt, his golden handsomeness in radiant evidence. But his cowboy hotness is marred by a white, bloodstained T-shirt pressed to his forehead.

Great.

Patrick sighs. Now his day has really gone completely off the runners. "Just think. If I'd only let all those cancer kids keel over dead, I'd be working somewhere warm year round right now," he mutters. "And there would be no Pattersons or Molinaros or honeymoons interrupting my life."

Jenny frowns. "And no Will either. And no me."

Kimberly spots him as he groans softly. "Help. I can't shake them. They're everywhere."

"What? Who?" Jenny asks, her brows knitting in confusion, looking around.

"Them."

"Patrick!" Kimberly calls, waving. Her dress swirls

around her cowboy boots. Her face is pale and her blue eyes burn with worry. "Kevin's had an accident. We need you."

"Oh." Jenny's brows jump up and she tightens her ponytail again. "I see what you mean."

"Will's perfect ass makes it all worth it," he reminds himself under his breath as he rises and grimaces his acknowledgement to Kimberly.

Will's ass, and his smile, and the way he rubs at his face when his BG is dropping, and how Patrick feels when Will looks at him like he's something special.

There are all kinds of things about Will that make it worth it.

Before he loses his chance, he turns to Jenny and gives his two cents. "Don't let your snobbery get in the way of the best orgasms you've ever had in your life."

She snorts at him.

He waves toward his in-laws. "I didn't and look at me. Happy family."

"Oh, yeah. Right. Happy family indeed." She laughs.

Patrick doesn't argue but says, "Tom is bad news. Make up with Jax." Then he heads down the corridor toward Kimberly and Kevin.

The ponytailed brunette nurse he yelled at earlier is back at the station. He wonders where Varun has scampered off to right when he needs him the most. "Get this man a room and schedule an emergency CT STAT."

"But he hasn't been through admitting or the ER,

Dr. McCloud."

"Why would we?" Kimberly says, eyes widening in offence. "My son-in-law is the head neurosurgeon in this hospital! The best of the best!"

Patrick wishes he could record her saying that and then turn back time to play it for her on the day they first met. "You heard her," Patrick says to the nurse. "The best of the best."

The nurse's lips thin but she forces a smile.

"Get him in a room," Patrick orders. "I'll deal with the fallout."

"Hospital procedure dictates—"

"I'm sure you know me well enough by now to know what you can do with hospital procedure."

"But Varun—"

"You're not Varun."

She blanches. "Room 8-F is empty."

"And now it's not."

Let the people in admitting pitch a fit. Let Don Knife tell him he has to follow the rules or get lightly slapped on the wrist. Let his other patients wait an hour for his attention even though it's not fair.

Life's not fair.

He has a Patterson to take care of.

He grips Kevin's arm and steers him toward the room. Kevin's face is pale and his grayish-green eyes are slightly dilated. He's also docile as a deer, and obviously disoriented. The idiots should have called an ambulance.

"From what I can tell," Kimberly starts once they're

in the room, "Kevin was bucked from a stallion he's been training." She helps Kevin sit on the bed.

Patrick presses his thumb and forefinger to his eyes. It's almost like they're children. "And you didn't think to call 911?"

"They'd turn us over to just any doctor. He needs *you*."

Patrick stares at his mother-in-law. Kimberly's laying it on a bit thick even for her. He's not even supposed to treat relatives. Hospital procedure. Regardless, he examines Kevin carefully and asks him questions about the accident.

Kevin grimaces. "I was on Sunburst, my newest stallion. I'd taken him out to work on jumps. I don't remember what happened. I just know I lost my seat."

Patrick shines his penlight in Kevin's eyes, making note of any evidence of injury. "Could be a concussion. We'll know more after the CT."

Kimberly nudges in closer. "I found him wandering up from the field with blood all over his face and neck." Her hand finds her brother's and grips hard. "I got him in the car and brought him straight to you."

Patrick grunts. Does she want him to praise her for quick thinking? Uh, no. Her failure to call for an ambulance could have cost her brother his life.

Still, at this point, he can't read her the riot act because he's fairly sure Kevin's going to be just fine. And if he *does* give her an earful, just for the principle of the thing, she'll probably panic, decide Kevin is dying, and start them down a whole path of drama-rama that Patrick just doesn't have time for right now.

"I didn't text Will about this yet," Kimberly says. Then a gleam comes to her eye. "Will you do it?"

Patrick doesn't know what's up with her. There's something going on, some convoluted plan, and he can't put a finger on it. The Patterson-Molinaro family's machinations are annoying and often ridiculous. "I have other patients," he snaps. "Text him yourself."

Kimberly frowns slightly, but then her lips quirk up at the corner. "Suit yourself."

Patrick jerks open the door to the room, sees Varun passing by, and grabs his arm. "Get in here. I need you to do the intake on this patient. He bypassed admitting."

"How?"

Patrick waves off his questions. "He has a head wound, probable concussion, and requires a CT STAT, followed by SCAT-2 assessment, neurological assessment, and constant monitoring until he can get down to imaging."

"Constant monitoring?" Varun asks, acidly.

"Did I stutter?"

Varun glares at him, but doesn't argue. He bustles in and puts on that great nurse-smile of his that people love, and his dark eyes fill with warmth for Kevin and Kimberly as he greets them.

"Ah, I see!" He shoots Patrick a smart-ass look over his shoulder and then turns back to Kevin. "It's Mr. Patterson and Ms. Patterson. That explains a lot."

"How so?" Kimberly asks.

"You're getting very special treatment, that's all."

Kimberly smiles.

"Let me get you comfortable in a gown, Mr. Patterson, and we'll assess the situation."

Kimberly relaxes as Varun chats, asks pertinent questions about the injury, and helps Kevin start to undress. This is the exact reason why Varun should get paid enough to come on full time. He's a dream with patients.

Patrick nods a curt goodbye to Kimberly and calls out, "You're in good hands, Kevin. Do what the pretty nurse says. And Varun, I meant what I told you. Eyes on this one constantly."

Varun gives him a saccharine and completely insincere smile. "Anything for your family, Doc."

"Will's family," he corrects. "And damn straight you'll do anything for them." He sends a glare Kimberly's way. "Because I'll never hear the end of it from him if I let one of these idiots die."

"Patrick!" Kimberly snaps.

Satisfied that he's offended his mother-in-law enough, he leaves the room with a flick of his white lab coat.

Stalking toward Don Knife's office to renew his effort to destroy the career of the drug-withholding Ruby-what's-her-face, he decides to stir the pot on *The Hurting Times* gossip forums.

He can't post that Kevin's been injured, not without breaking doctor-patient confidentiality, but he has plenty of other things to complain about. Patrick knows exactly how he'll start his post.

Logging in to *The Hurting Times* app as Dr. HottieMcBrainSurgeon, he types with his thumbs as he walks:

> *It's a truth universally acknowledged that the Pattersons of Healing, South Dakota are massive drama queens and total pains in my ass. And, no, I'm not posting about Will this time.*

Chapter Four

"**S**O, YOU'RE ALL packed up, Caity-bug," Will murmurs, kicking at the suitcases by his sister's feet.

It's a beautiful late summer day with a cool breeze, and they're standing in the driveway with the dark gray clapboard and stone two-story house they grew up in looming behind them. It's the place where they lived through their mom's endless relationship dramas, where they grieved the loss of Caitlin's father, Roger, and from which both of them have always been eager to escape.

Will admires his sister in the crisp afternoon light. She's beautiful, with buttery hair that's styled loose and free, falling down either side of her shoulders to frame her buxom chest. Her flower-patterned sundress is topped with a light sweater, and she's wearing cowboy boots. Like their mom.

She's always been soft and rounded, and as she's grown up that hasn't changed. But now she's woman where a little girl used to be, and Will can't believe how beautiful she looks.

"It took forever to whittle it down to just these suitcases, but I think I have everything I really need." She smiles tremulously at him with the blue sky reflected in her eyes. It's just the two of them since Olivia and Connor are at school, having already told Caitlin goodbye over breakfast.

"We can ship anything you've forgotten. Or you can buy what you need out there. Don't worry about money."

She slips her arm around his waist and half-hugs him. "Thanks. You and Nonna are being really good to me. Mom's being…" She rolls her eyes. "Mom."

He doesn't point out that while their mother is a mess, Caitlin doesn't make it any easier when she blocks Kimberly from her life the way she tends to do. He doesn't say it because Patrick tells him that kind of comment "enables the abuser"—wherein the abuser is Kimberly—and that Will needs to stop defending his mother when she's being indefensible. It's a thing he's working on.

"Yeah. I know how she can be. Feeling scared?"

"Not so much *scared*, but…"

"Not exactly ready to go out in the big wide world all alone, either?"

Caitlin's lower lip wobbles, and she throws herself into his arms. "I'm so ready to get away from here. Mom makes me crazy," she whispers, her voice clogged with tears. "So why am I crying? It's not like I'm *scared* to leave home, but…but it's still my home, you know?"

Will hugs her for a long time, smoothing his hand

through her hair, breathing in her scent. He remembers when his mom brought her home from the hospital. She'd smelled so fresh and new. Now she smells like fruity perfume.

"You've worked hard for this. You're going to be great out there. I'm proud of you and you don't need to worry about anything going on here at home. Mom, Uncle Kevin, Patrick, and I can hold down the fort."

"I know you can, but I feel so guilty dumping the kids on you." She pulls free of his arms and wipes at her eyes. Her mascara smudges, but she gets it on the next pass. "You took care of me all these years, and I know I'm skipping out on paying you back."

"Oh, Caity-bug, no. I didn't take care of you so you'd eventually do the same for Olivia and Connor. I want you to grow into your best self, and if that means going to Colorado for school, then that's all I want for you."

Will can't blame Caitlin for choosing to go so far away from their crazy family, but he really *is* going to miss her. Olivia and Connor will miss her too. And not just for her chauffeuring and babysitting skills. He knows she's been the one keeping the household together since he and Patrick married.

He'll do his best to keep things sane for them. In the end, it'll likely be Olivia's turn to step up and help care for Connor until she flees the nest too.

"Really? You're not mad? Even a little?" The breeze whips at them. He smells a hint of rain coming in.

"Not even a little." He tucks her hair behind her ear.

"How are Olivia and Connor taking things?"

"Olivia says she's happy I'm leaving so she can get my room."

"That's a lie. She's going to miss you."

"I know. And Connor is angry." Her lips twist. "I know he's just nine, but…"

"Remember how angry Olivia was with me when I went to school?"

Caitlin laughs. "I remember. She got all the socks that you'd left behind, doused them in lighter fluid, and burned them in a giant pile out here on the driveway. You can still see the scorch marks." She points at a blackened area near the basketball net.

"But she got over it."

"Eventually." Caitlin eyes him pensively.

"What?"

"It's just strange remembering that time. Back when you were with Ryan."

"Oh. Yeah." Will clears his throat. He gazes up at the sky and sees darker clouds edging onto the horizon. "That feels like another life."

She nods slowly. "Do you ever hear from him?"

Will shakes his head. A slither of guilt tries to worm in, telling him he *should* know what's happening with his ex, his first love, his first everything. But he shoves the thoughts away ruthlessly. "I haven't seen or heard from him in a very long time."

"Oh." She lowers her brows and stares over his shoulder, her expression saying she knows something and she's not sure whether she should tell him.

He licks his lips. "I hope he's happy wherever he is."

She nods and clears her throat, eyes darting to the ground as she crosses her arms. The sky is quiet as the dark, fat clouds roll closer. The silence between them grows and he knows whatever news she's holding back, it's not good.

"What have you heard?" he eventually whispers.

"Not much." She meets his eyes, and her own are full of empathy. "Hartley came back into town for his dad's funeral and he looks pretty bad. And not just from grief. He looks...bad."

"I know." Well, he didn't know Hartley had been in town recently, but the last time he saw him still haunts his dreams. Hartley had been a shell of the proud man he'd been before he left town with Ryan. And Will still thinks the shadows under his eyes were healing bruises.

"Ryan wasn't with him when I ran into him at Brown Gargle. But Andy Sicko told me later that Hartley told *him* Ryan's in the hospital."

Will swallows hard.

"Yeah," Caitlin whispers. "With acute liver failure from drinking. They're trying to get him on a transplant list, but it doesn't look good."

Will breathes in and out slowly. As far as the whole reel-him-in-and-then-clock-him-with-a-two-by-four act goes, Caitlin's just as good as Kimberly, apparently. "I see. That...that sucks."

"Yeah. But I don't understand. Ryan never drank

when he was with *you*."

"No." Will shakes his head.

While they were together, Ryan hadn't ever had a drop as far as Will knew. Instead he just drove Will to drink, taking some kind of addictive, abusive pleasure in hurting Will, undermining him, and setting him up to fail.

"I wonder why he started drinking again after you broke up?"

Will shivers. He doesn't want to think about these things. He doesn't want to know. He swallows with an audible click and stuffs his hands into his pockets, rocking back and forth on his heels, trying to regain his balance.

"Do you think he couldn't forget you?" Caitlin asks, gently.

"No," Will whispers. "I think he's an alcoholic."

"So are you. And now that you're with Patrick, you don't drink anymore, either."

Will wipes a hand over his mouth. "It's not like it's always easy. It's not like I don't have to make a daily effort to stay sober. I didn't fall in love with Patrick and wake up cured."

"I know. But you're so much happier with Patrick. Doesn't that help?"

"Yes. It helps. But it doesn't mean I never struggle with it."

The lines between her brows deepen. "Maybe Ryan wasn't as happy with Hartley. Maybe that's why—"

"Stop!" Will puts his hand on Caitlin's shoulder and squeezes. He swallows down swelling nausea. "I can't think about things like that, Caitlin. I can't be responsible for him."

"Oh! I didn't mean you were!" Her eyes go wide, and he believes she hadn't intended that implication. "I just…never mind. I should have kept my mouth shut."

Will smiles, but his gut churns. "It's okay. I was bound to find out anyway."

"I'm surprised Patrick didn't tell you. It *has* to be all over that *Hurting Times* app he loves so much."

Will rubs a hand over his suddenly sweaty forehead. No doubt Patrick does know all about Ryan's situation and Hartley's visit. But Patrick also knows Will too well and loves him too much to think he needs to hear anything about it.

He'll want to protect Will from these feelings surging inside of him now. He'll want to keep Will from thinking about the Tallgrass bar and how easy it can be to stop by there on the way home.

Patrick understands Will better than Caitlin or Kimberly or Kevin ever will. The real surprise here is that Kimberly hasn't told him already. Surely she knows? Maybe she finally believes him when he says that Ryan was abusive? Or maybe she's just tired of that particular fight? He has no idea.

Will tries to change the subject back to something safe. Back to Caitlin and her future. "What time are you heading out?"

"In an hour. Nonna and Reba are picking me up, and then Nonna is flying out with me." She chews on her bottom lip. "Where's Mom? She said she'd be here. She's supposed to bring Uncle Kevin from the farm with her to say goodbye to me too."

Will rubs her arms. "She'll be here. They'll both be here. Like Uncle Kevin would let you go without hugging his Caity-bug."

"I know, it's just... She makes me crazy. Sometimes I doubt things I shouldn't ever have a reason to doubt."

Will laughs. "I know. Me too."

He leads her over to the shaded side porch and takes her suitcases in case it starts to rain. Then they sit on the loveseat glider Kimberly put out a few years ago.

Taking her hand, he threads her fingers with his own. "I'm glad Nonna is going out to Colorado with you. She'll make sure your dorm room is set up in style."

Caitlin snorts. "Mom's pissed about it. She wanted to take me herself, but I told her no. I don't want her ruining it for me, you know?"

Will nods.

"She and Nonna fought about it."

"I bet they did."

"Nonna and I won."

Will nods and slings his arm over Caitlin's shoulder. The loveseat glides back and forth slowly. "As if anyone could defeat the combined forces of Eleanora Molinaro and Caitlin Flemings-Patterson."

They rock in silence for a while. Will lets his worries

about Ryan and his urge for a drink drift away like the dark clouds across the sky. The smell of rain passes as the plains pull the sky toward the west. It's been over two years since his last drink. He's happily married and getting ready to head out on a much-belated honeymoon. Getting drunk now would jeopardize so much more than he's ever had to lose before. He doesn't need it.

He wants it.

But he doesn't need it.

Finally, Caitlin murmurs, "Everyone else's parents will be there and I'll just have Nonna. She's not even my real grandmother. She's yours."

Their mother's twisted and doomed relationships have left them all with a hodge-podge of convoluted family members, and Will's biological father has left him with even more.

"That doesn't mean Nonna doesn't love you."

"I know."

"Because she does."

"I *know.*" She flips her hair impatiently.

"Do you want me to go with you?"

"No! You need to get ready for your trip with Patrick. Besides, I don't want my brother there. I want my mom. Get it? But she's…" Caitlin waves her hands around. "I hate that I feel so mixed-up about this."

"Feeling mixed-up about Mom means you're sane." Will thinks about the guilt that's been stamped on his heart since breakfast. "She's good at making us doubt ourselves.”

As their time together draws to a close, Will gets out his wallet and hands Caitlin a couple hundreds. “Take these. Once you and Nonna set up a bank account, I’ll wire you an allowance every month. Be responsible with it.”

“Seriously?”

“I believe in you, Caitlin.”

She hugs him tightly and struggles with tears again, tight little puffs of wet breath hitting his neck. He fights off his own. Eventually, she whispers, “You need to go?”

“Yeah. I’m sorry I can’t wait for Nonna and Reba with you.” Though he isn’t sad about missing his mother again.

As if on cue, Will’s phone vibrates and he sighs to see that Owen, his right-hand man at Good Works, requires his presence back at the office to sign a ton of papers before he leaves town himself. “I have to go, but I’m always here for you. Always. I’m just text or call away. Or come home if you really need to, okay? You’re always welcome home.”

“Thank you.” She hugs him again and Will clutches her tightly. “Have fun in…” She frowns. “Where are you two going?”

Will smiles. “It’s a secret.”

Caitlin grins. “Oh, okay. Good plan. Don’t let Mom find out the details or she’ll find some way to make your honeymoon all about her. I want to hear everything when you get back, okay?”

"We can FaceTime."

Caitlin kisses his cheek, and he squeezes her hand. "You're gonna be amazing out there," he tells her again.

"Get in your car and go, cheeseball. Jeez." She shoves him playfully. "You're getting borderline ridiculous now."

Will blows her another kiss as he climbs into his BMW and heads back into town. He knows Caitlin's future will be bright, but a tug in his gut tells him nothing is ever going to be the same once she crosses the town line.

She'll have flown.

"WILL ISN'T ANSWERING his texts or his phone." Kimberly tosses her phone back into her blue Christian Louboutin purse. "Neither is Caitlin. What if he's drinking? What if she's dead in a ditch?"

Patrick ignores her. If there's a problem with Will's blood sugar, even a big insulin dump like one required to cover the onslaught of a bunch of alcoholic drinks, his phone will get a notification from the monitor. If Will wants to turn off his phone to avoid the drama llama that is his mother, that's his prerogative. Patrick wishes he could turn off his *reality* to avoid it himself.

He checks Kevin's pupils and reflexes, and reviews the SCAT-2 findings again. The concussion is mild, but he's not taking chances with his uncle-in-law.

"Will's probably in a meeting," Kevin says sensibly. "I don't need him here. Honestly, Kimberly, I don't need you here either. I'm fine. Go on home."

"I already missed saying goodbye to Caitlin," she says morosely.

Kevin sighs. "That was your choice. I told you I was fine here alone."

"You're not fine, Kevin! You could have a brain bleed and die. Do you understand?" Her eyes go annoyingly wide. "Die! And what would I do without you?"

Kevin sighs.

Patrick raises his brow and sends what he hopes is a sympathetic look but it's probably more of a "your sister is cray-cray, and you're marginally less dumb than I thought" look instead. He's apparently good at those.

Kevin rolls his eyes, and Patrick's not sure if that's for Kimberly or him.

Kimberly's phone dings and she gasps. "It's Caitlin. They were in the air when I texted. They just landed to make their connection. She's angry. I need to call her."

Patrick slaps the sign on the wall by the bed. "Out."

"What?"

He slaps the sign again. "No cell phones. Out."

"That's absurd. I've seen you use your cell phone in these rooms. No one pays attention to those signs."

"Unless you want these monitors to miss something important about your brother that could lead to him being a brain-dead zombie by dinnertime, then get out of this hospital room. You can use your phone on one of the outdoor decks or at an entrance."

Kimberly glares at him, huffs as she pulls her purse over her shoulder, and marches out with a toss of her blond head.

"She's been on that phone all day," Kevin says, scrubbing a hand over his jaw, worry threading his voice.

"The sign's crap. I needed a break."

Kevin barks a soft laugh. "Oh. Well, thanks. I needed a break too."

Patrick shares a smile with the man who once tried to convince Will not to stay married to him and who'd been completely snowed by Ryan Whitehead for years. Time mends all wounds, apparently.

"What's the diagnosis, doc?" Kevin asks.

"Mild concussion. I'm going to keep you here overnight for observation. There's no evidence of anything to worry about, but I want to be safe." Or risk Will's wrath if something happens to his uncle.

Kevin's eyes go thoughtful. "Will the nurse who was in earlier be here tonight?"

Patrick lifts a brow, smirking. "No, Varun's left for the day, but the night nurses aren't absolute idiots, so I think you'll be fine."

"Thanks. I wish I remembered what happened. And I hope Sunburst moseyed on home. There's no one I really trust to bring him back in."

"He's a horse on a horse farm. He'll be fine."

Kevin nods. "So, about that nurse…"

"Yes, he's gay and available."

Kevin's face floods red. "I…didn't…he…"

"He's pretty. I understand."

"He's not…" Kevin grows even redder. "I'm not interested in him like that. I just wanted to say that you seem overly familiar with him, and vice versa. Frankly, I want to believe there's nothing happening there, but I can't say it didn't cross my mind."

Patrick guffaws. "Puh-lease. He's got gorgeous eyes, but he's not Will."

"And he's not Roy," Kevin says, his lips tilting up and his gray-green eyes shading sad.

Patrick nods. "Understood."

"Yes, well. Good. I just needed to be sure. Will's been through enough in his life."

Patrick barely keeps back a snarling comment about how a lot of that suffering was because Kevin and Kimberly didn't see Ryan for the abusive jerk he really was, but he keeps it in and gives himself a thousand bonus points. He must have leveled up in the social skills department, because a year ago, he'd have let it rip.

"Speaking of Will," he says, backing away from Kevin's hospital bed. "I need to get home. You rest up. Do what the nurses say and you can most likely get back to the farm tomorrow morning."

Kevin leans back, the blue gown making his eyes look slate-gray. "Thanks for your help today. I know it made Kimberly feel better that you were the one treating me."

"Anything for a Patterson." Patrick throws open the door, heading out into the quiet hallway. It's early evening, and he's done all the damage he can do at the hospital. He's ready for home and Will.

Chapter Five

W ILL DROPS HIS keys into the basket on the shelf by the door to the garage and takes a long, slow breath. The soft light-green walls and cream trim of the kitchen opens up to the warm earth tones of the hallway.

Summer's evening light filters in from the wide windows by the kitchen table, illuminating the sparkling marble counter tops and stainless steel appliances. His shoulders relax.

Home. It's his favorite place to be.

Crossing to the broad, dark wood table, he unloads the bags he's picked up from Jimmy's, their local diner, onto the counter. He's brought mac 'n' joe, Patrick's favorite, and a hamburger and fries for himself. He worked out earlier in the day at the new gym he installed in the Good Works offices, so he feels justified in flooding his body with high calorie, fatty, delicious diner food.

The sound of their piano drifts to the kitchen from the living room as he unpacks the bags. Will pauses with his hip against the counter to listen. As the music slips over him, his muscles relax and even his hair seems to settle more gently against his scalp. The knot of sadness he's felt since his conversation with Caitlin about Ryan loosens and he can breathe smoothly again. Then the music shifts.

He cocks his head, a smile floating on his lips.

Patrick plays a pop song that's been ear-worming everyone and their brother the last few weeks. The chorus is passionate and plaintive, a lover calling desperately to the one she's lost. Patrick pounds the keys on those parts, and Will shivers, the emotion radiating from the song.

Still, he's surprised Patrick's willingly playing it. He knows how much Patrick loathes this particular singer, calling her sultry voice "ridiculous," and her fashion sense "demented."

Regardless, Will loves how Patrick can instinctively pick up nearly anything he hears, especially now that he's finally back in practice after years of abandoning the piano due to his father's abuse.

Will listens a bit longer and then goes back to unpacking their dinner. The scents make his mouth water.

"Puddin'-pop," Patrick calls. "Get in here and do something to get this hideous song out of my head."

"You get in here and eat dinner with me," he calls back.

A few seconds later, a tired and disgruntled Patrick strolls into the room. His always neat, curly auburn hair looks as though he's been dragging his hands through it, and he's got a reddish five o'clock shadow going on.

He's barefoot and wearing the black jeans he prefers with the same rust-colored button-down shirt he owns four of.

"Mac 'n'joe?" he asks, sharp blue eyes scanning the take-out containers as he sniffs the air.

"Of course."

"Thank Christ."

"It's been that kind of day, huh?" Will wads up the paper bags the food came in and throws them in the recycle container.

"For you too?"

Will nods. He doesn't want to bring up what his sister told him about Ryan, though. That's still a sore spot with Patrick, if only because Will can't seem to stop caring about Ryan, deep down. He's not in love with the guy anymore. Not in a very long time. But he does retain basic human caring for his first love.

Will knows Patrick's not jealous. He just doesn't think what Will does to himself when the subject of Ryan comes up is healthy. And given how guilty and nauseous he's felt off and on all day since Caitlin told him about Ryan being in the hospital, dying, Patrick's probably right.

They gather the dishes and silverware as a team and sit down to dig into their dinner.

"How'd it go with Caitlin?" Patrick asks, eventually. "She seemed excited when she called me yesterday to say goodbye."

Will sighs. "She's never coming back."

"Nope."

"You're supposed to reassure me."

"Why would I do that? She's not coming back." Patrick jabs the air with his fork. "I wouldn't come back if I were her." He chews another giant bite of mac'n'joe and moans softly. "This is good."

"You say that every time."

"Because it's good every time. And, you're right. I should reassure you. But I can't. Your sister isn't the brightest bulb in the Patterson family chandelier, but she's smart enough to leave and never return." He wipes his mouth with a napkin. "It's a no-brainer to get far away from Healing and, more to the point, Kimberly."

Will takes a bite of his burger and swallows before saying, "Mom's not that bad."

"Oh, yes she is."

"I know, but…" Will squirms in his seat. "She's my mother."

"More's the pity." He zeroes in on Will now. "She got under your skin this morning, huh?"

Will squeezes ketchup over his fries and pops two in his mouth. "I don't know how she does it, but she always manages to make me feel guilty. Like I haven't earned the right to do what I want with my life."

"You've more than earned everything you have."

"I know. She just…" Will shakes it off, taking another bite of burger. "Let's not talk about her. How was your day?"

Patrick makes a noise of disgust, shoves in more of

his dinner, and shrugs. "Just another day in paradise."

"How'd your morning surgery go?"

"Canceled. Patient popped a fever."

"So that's why you're grumpy." Will smiles. "Didn't get to mess around in anyone's brains today."

Patrick lightly snarls. "I've got plenty of reasons to be grumpy. Your family is annoying and the nurses here are criminals."

Will almost chokes on his laugh. "The nurses are *what?*"

"Criminals."

"Okay, back up."

Patrick wipes his mouth and launches into a long and irritated tale of a nurse he suspects of charting a dose of anti-seizure medication without actually giving it to a patient. The entire rant takes long enough for them both to finish their meal and move from the table to the cushy sofa in the living room.

The housekeeper came during the day, so the remote controls are lined up carefully on the broad coffee table and the TV screen and windows onto their wide, summer-green backyard shine dust-free and spotless.

"Her name's Ruby something," Patrick sums up with a glare, like the name means everything. He turns to prop his bare feet up in Will's lap. "She's new and a redhead. Never trust a redhead."

"You and Connor are both redheads."

"I bet she's a Sagittarius too. I'd put money on it." Patrick taps his fingers anxiously against his left leg even as he stretches out to get more settled on the couch.

"Patrick, has it occurred to you that you're fixating on this woman?"

Fixation sometimes happens with Patrick's autism spectrum disorder. His brain locates an "enemy" and he can't let it go until he's solved the problem or defeated the brain tumor or whatever else.

"Now you sound like Don," Patrick grumbles. He wriggles his toes and Will gives in, massaging his feet. "Ah, that's more like it."

"So you talked to Don about the nurse?"

"Of course. Ruby what's-her-face needs to get out of my hospital. Yesterday."

Will digs into the arch of Patrick's left foot. "Okay, so how did that conversation go?"

Don Knife is a big fan of Patrick's, so Will's betting it went reasonably well, but he's also a fair man, so he isn't going to let Patrick's suspicions ruin a woman's career untested.

Patrick rolls his eyes. "It went annoyingly, of course. I told him what I told you, plus I asked him how I'm supposed to feel comfortable leaving my patients for ten days when the nurses are charting medications they never gave."

"What did he say?"

"Something about not getting ahead of ourselves and how we need to wait for the lab results on my patient's urine. As if I don't know what she looks like on five hundred milligrams of Keppra versus zero." Patrick hisses as Will hits a tender spot on his heel.

"Don's hands are tied until he has proof."

Patrick closes his eyes and tilts his head back, relaxing a little as Will works on the tender areas of his feet. "I realize that."

Will ponders the situation as he continues the foot massage. "If she didn't give the dose but she charted it, what did she even do with the meds? It's not like there's a lot of demand on the dark and disturbing streets of Healing for Keppra."

"Maybe out on the reservation. Folks out there have a hard time getting the medications they need from Indian Health Services. They have to travel a long way. It can be dangerous or impossible for someone with seizures to get a ride all the way to Eagle Butte for an appointment. That's a problem. It needs to be fixed. The folks on the reservation deserve health care."

"They do."

"Still, this Ruby can't just—"

"Patrick. Let's wait for the urine. Maybe your patient is metabolizing faster than she should be."

Patrick's brows furrow. "In that case, another MRI will be needed to see if there's something going on with her liver or—"

"Right. And that's not something that can't be handled in your absence. Calm down. Don and Dr. Lerma will be able to deal with everything while we're away."

Patrick nods once, sharply. His fingers tap on his pant leg again and his lips narrow into a straight, hard line. "It's a crime."

"If she's stealing drugs, then Don will handle it. It doesn't have to be up to you."

Patrick harrumphs and stares off over Will's shoulder, his blue eyes narrowing in thought. "She's messing with my patient."

"I know."

They sit in silence for a while until Patrick pulls his feet away and motions at Will. "Your turn."

Kicking off his shoes and toeing off his socks, Will lets out a long sigh before depositing his feet in Patrick's lap. He's not on his feet all day the way Patrick is, but he never turns down a *quid pro quo* foot rub.

He groans and lets his head fall back against the couch cushions as Patrick's long, steady, surgeon's fingers dig into the balls of his feet and work through the tender areas.

He can tell by the way Patrick's eyes search the air around them that he's still thinking about the nurse and trying to solve the problem. In the quiet of their living room, evening shadows grow long. His own mind drifts back to the driveway and the sunlight shining in Caitlin's hair as she'd told him about Ryan.

He licks his lips, opens his mouth, and shuts it again. Scrunching his eyes tightly, he tries to let Patrick's fingers work their magic, but still he can't let go of the mental image of Ryan: skin yellow, eyes sunken, wired to machines in the hospital and waiting to die. He rubs his eyes hard, trying to drive the image away.

"If she's hurting my patient, she deserves punishment," Patrick mutters.

Will's throat goes dry, an idea coming to mind—a way to block out his guilty thoughts and distract Patrick from obsessing. He clears his throat.

"Want to punish someone?" Will asks, unbuttoning the top button of his shirt and exposing a stripe of his chest hair.

Patrick's gaze swerves his way.

Will smiles and undoes another button, revealing even more of the fur he knows Patrick loves so well. "I know someone who enjoys being spanked. He might be willing to play bad nurse. If you want."

Patrick's lips soften and his blue eyes dilate slowly. "Does that someone have a juicy ass that jiggles just the way I like?"

"I've heard he does."

"Prove it."

Will pulls his feet out of Patrick's hands and stands, disconnects his glucose monitor, and sheds his shirt before unbuckling his belt. Shoving his pants down, he spins around, arching his back slightly to display his naked ass. "How's this?"

"Hmm, I'm not sure." Patrick's warm hands cup his butt cheeks, and he lightly smacks the right one. "Yes, that's what I like." He does it again, a bit harder so it makes Will jump. "Just like that."

Will shivers, and his cock rises as he whispers. "Do you want me to play bad nurse?"

Patrick drags him back toward the couch and pulls him down onto his lap, chin hooking over his shoulder. "Mmm, no. Let's play captured superhero instead." He adjusts his hips so that beneath the soft material of his jeans his hard dick wedges between Will's ass cheeks.

Will laughs softly. Captured superhero is a silly game, but it'll crack the tension that'd been growing in the air. "Dr. Villain, I'll stop your evil plans."

Patrick slides his hands up Will's thighs, through his pubes, avoiding his hard cock, and then traces up to his stomach, sliding past his infusion site and BG sensor, then up to his nipples, tweaking them gently.

"You'll never make me come, Dr. Villain. Never," Will whispers and pretends to struggle against Patrick's hold. "I'll never break." His naked skin against Patrick's clothes is always a turn on and his cock flexes hard, bringing up a bubble of precome.

"We'll see about that, Super Do-Gooder." He maneuvers Will around so he's on his stomach, ass up, sprawled over Patrick's thighs. He slaps his ass gently at first, and Will wriggles around, trying to get him to do it harder. Patrick slaps him lightly again, and Will clutches the pillows in anticipation.

"You're weak, Dr. Villain," he says in his best superhero voice. "I'll defeat you yet."

"Weak?" Patrick smacks his butt harder and Will arches into it, barely holding back the cry of "yes" that wants to burst through his lips. "I'll show you weak, Super Do-Gooder." Then he lays a couple of good stinging whacks on Will's butt, grabbing it in both hands to squeeze greedily before spanking it again.

Will moans and grins into the pillow. "You're evil, Dr. Villain. Diabolical."

"You'll beg for mercy."

"Never."

"I'll make you beg to come."

"Never!"

Patrick sucks two of his own fingers into his mouth, gets them wet before prodding at Will's asshole firmly, gaining entrance as Will bears down to let him in. Patrick wriggles his fingers inside and Will groans. "Just as I suspected. A slut for it."

Will breaks into a sweat, and his voice is breathy when he says, "I'll never come for you! I'll resist to the end of time." But he lifts up his ass and takes Patrick's fingers in deeper.

When Patrick starts massaging his prostate, Will frantically rubs his cock against Patrick's too-soft jeans, mentally cursing that Patrick eschews the rougher fabrics.

"You're a dirty, filthy boy, Super Do-Gooder."

"I am!" Will groans, shoving back against Patrick's fingers. "I'm such a dirty boy."

Patrick laughs. "You love being fingered so much you can't even pretend to hate it."

Draped over Patrick's legs on the sofa, with his prostate shooting pleasure through his body, Will allows himself to disintegrate into a babbling, begging mess.

Patrick holds onto the game a bit longer.

"Just give me your dick, Patrick," Will whimpers. "Please."

"Poor, Super Do-Gooder. Look what you're reduced to. What would the good people of Healing think of you now?"

"Please," he whispers. "I want to come with you fucking me."

"What would they think to hear their superhero begging for Dr. Villain's fat cock like a slut?"

Will whimpers and bucks, trying to get enough friction on his dick. "Patrick."

"Yes, Super Do-Gooder?"

"Fuck me, you jerk."

Patrick chuckles and twists his fingers again just so. Will's cock aches and swells, and he humps Patrick's legs harder. "Please, Patr—"

Patrick tsks. "Uh-uh, Dr. Villain."

"Please Dr. Villain." Will's voice is rough and wet, the couch pillows are crumpled from his grip, and his asshole burns slightly from the spit-slicked finger fuck. "Make me come," he begs again. "Get your dick in me and make me come."

Patrick hisses and pulls his fingers free, wiping them on a tissue he grabs from the coffee table. Will flips over and clutches Patrick's face, kissing him passionately. Their tongues tangle, and Will slides from his position on Patrick's lap to the rug on the hardwood floor, tumbling Patrick down with him. Forcing Patrick's pants over his hips, Will's gratified when Patrick's cock flops out hard and slick at the tip.

He sucks it greedily, getting the taste of precome in his mouth. Then he falls to all fours, the rug scratchy beneath his knees, presenting his ass. He says over his shoulder, "Get your dick in me now, Dr. Villain."

Patrick spits liberally into his hand and wipes it over his cockhead before lining up with Will's asshole.

"Gonna burn," he whispers.

"Do it."

Pushing in, Patrick grunts. Will throws his head back, crooning with pleasure and pain. The burn from the rough entrance penetrates the haze of Will's lust, and he curses under his breath. Patrick pulls out again, reaches for the drawer in the coffee table, and grabs a stashed tube of lube. He applies it quickly, making Will shudder, then pushes in again, both of them crying out with pleasure.

"Yes," Will whispers as Patrick flattens himself against Will's back, shirt rough on his exposed and eager skin. "Pound me. I want it. I want you."

Patrick wraps his hands loosely around Will's exposed throat and goes to town, driving into him hard and fast. The sound of flesh slapping together and the scent of their fucking rises around them. Patrick grunts and whispers filthy things in Will's ear, and Will moans and writhes, trying to reach orgasm, hungry for it.

Patrick reaches around and takes hold of him. "Are you gonna come for me?" he growls, low and hot in

Will's ear.

"Yes!"

"Do it then."

"I'm close. Harder," Will demands, pushing back into each thrust, his body jolting with pleasure. "Now, please, hard. Harder." Patrick's hand tightens infinitesimally around his throat, claiming and possessive, commanding. "Yes! Oh, please!"

Will bites his lip, his body spasming and come shooting in bursts from his aching cock. He convulses hard beneath Patrick's still-thrusting body before he collapses, trembling, to the floor.

As Will heaves in breaths and shudders through aftershocks, Patrick grips Will's hips and slams into him, finally shoving in as far as he can, jerking as he comes too. His groan, broken and ragged, barely penetrates the sound of Will's thrumming pulse.

"And that's how Dr. Villain fucks Super Do-Gooder," Patrick mumbles in his ear after his own twitching has stopped.

Will laughs softly, his limbs already protesting the rough floor sex. A niggle of reality forms in the back of his mind about the mess they'll have to clean up.

Patrick pulls out slowly, pushing whatever small amount of come slips out back in. He collapses on the floor beside Will and draws him close.

"That was great," Will murmurs, dreamy and tired now. The things he's been trying to avoid thinking about have drifted away in the bliss of post-sex recovery in

Patrick's arms.

"By the way," Patrick says, his voice gravelly from all the groaning. "Your uncle's going to be fine."

"Hmm?"

"Your mom didn't text you?"

"Text me about what?" He's had his phone off ever since he went into the meeting with Owen, mainly so he wouldn't have to listen to his mother's hysterics over his sister leaving. He just didn't have the energy for her after hearing about Ryan.

Crap. Ryan.

"Your uncle's in the hospital with a concussion. Overnight for observation. He's fine."

Will sits up, knocking Patrick's arm off. "I had no idea. I should…we should…"

Patrick slides a reassuring hand up Will's arm and shakes his head. "Nope. We should clean up, read in bed, and get some sleep. Like I said, he's fine."

Will sighs and rubs his face. Patrick frowns, considering him carefully for a moment. "Hook yourself back up. Test. I'll be back with some fruit juice."

Will replaces the tubing for his monitor and pump, puts his underwear back on so he clip the pump to it, and waits. Patrick returns with fruit juice. Will sips it while Patrick pricks his finger for the test.

"A little low, but you'll be fine."

Will nods and rubs at his face. "I feel a little woozy. Is the sensor in all right?"

Patrick un-tapes the sensor on Will's abdomen carefully and withdraws it. "I don't know. Let's put in a new one to be sure."

Sipping his juice, Will lets Patrick handle the trade for him. He's tired after the sex and drained now that he's remembered about Ryan, and his low BG isn't helping his mood any. Once Patrick finishes double-taping everything back and Will's juice box is drained, they clear up the mess they made before going upstairs to shower.

"Do you not want to go on the trip?" Will asks, washing his hair and watching Patrick soap up under the second showerhead across from him.

Patrick frowns. "Why?"

"Earlier, you made it sound like you were worried about going, because of having to trust your patients with the other doctors."

"I've planned this trip down to the last detail. We're going."

"But it won't be fun if you're going to panic about it."

"Panic is a strong word. I'll be stressed about it. But I promised you a honeymoon and you'll have a honey-moon."

Will smiles, but his heart isn't totally in it. Maybe he's being selfish to go away right now. Maybe he should drive to Vermillion and make sure Ryan's getting good medical care. Maybe his mom does need his help with the kids, and what if Patrick's wrong about Kevin being okay?

"Hey, don't you panic now," Patrick says, closing in, soap glistening on his skin and his blue eyes knowing in a way that makes Will shiver. "We're going on a honeymoon, and no one, not even ourselves, will get in the way of it. Understand?"

Will's smile is wobbly, but he knows Patrick's right. "Got it."

Almost an hour and a half later, Patrick sleeps cradled against his chest, and Will wishes he'd talked with him about Ryan after all. He wants to hear him say, "It's not your fault." Sometimes he has a hard time believing that simple truth.

He drops a kiss on the top of Patrick's head, digs deep, finding the strength in himself to push away the guilt. He hopes one day he'll fully accept that he can't fix everything and everyone.

He's only a pretend superhero.

PART TWO

Chapter Six

"DID YOU TEXT Dinah?" Will paws through a stack of Good Works contracts and papers he's brought along for the trip on the private jet. They've reached cruising altitude, and the pilot has given the okay for them to relax.

"Yep. I texted her this morning." Patrick closes his eyes and hopes the Xanax he's popped kicks in soon. He hates heights and flying in particular. Worse, this trip is going to be ridiculously long. Why didn't he and Jenny choose a closer location? Like, say, within driving distance? North Dakota is surely perfectly nice this time of year.

"And?" Will prompts.

"And the adoption is going through for Eric."

"That's great! Dinah and Phil must be ecstatic."

"They are." Patrick sits up straighter and glances at Will, outlined by the sun through the window. "Jane is upset, though, because she doesn't understand why they can't adopt her too."

"Let me guess. Her bio-mom keeps pulling that same last-minute crap?"

"Months without contact and then, right before child abandonment laws kick in, she shows up."

"Evil."

"She loves her daughter," Patrick mutters. "But not enough to leave her for good."

Patrick feels the echo of his own family pain rise around them. His father was an alcoholic who never got over his mother's death. He'd used Patrick's talent at the piano to earn money for bottles and to pay the rent. When that wasn't enough, he'd been willing to let Patrick prostitute himself.

That was when Patrick turned himself in to Child Protection Services and ended up a foster kid with Phil and Dinah. Bad memories taste like chalk and he swallows them down with a bitter grimace.

Finally, the moment passes and Will says, "I hope you gave Dinah, Phil, and the kids my love."

Patrick shrugs. "Why would I? They know you love them."

Will rolls his eyes but laughs softly. Then he turns to peer out the window at the fat clouds passing by.

So long as Patrick doesn't look down, or think about the fact that only lift, thrust, and drag are keeping them alive right now, he does okay. In fact, the clouds out the window almost make things better. Like he could step out onto them and have a nap in the sun.

He frowns. Will's fanciful thinking is wearing off on him. Or maybe it's the Xanax.

"So that nurse was let go?" Will asks quietly. "I heard

you on the phone with Don earlier. It's only been, what, three days? They found the evidence quickly."

"Yep. I was right, of course. I always am."

"So what does that mean for her?"

"Charges are being pressed." Patrick wrinkles his nose. "It's out of my hands now."

Will nods and sighs. "People make such bad choices sometimes." He shivers slightly, and Patrick checks to see if the air vent above them is open too far. "What did she do with the drugs she didn't administer to your patient?"

"She was hoarding what she could get to take it out to the rez. Indian Health Services is crap."

"I know. But let's not get into the American government's broken promises to the Native peoples today. It's too depressing and we're on vacation."

Patrick frowns. "That's right. Vacation. Just you and me for ten days." He takes hold of Will's hand. "You'll be sick of me by then."

"Never." Will's brown eyes take on a gleam and Patrick's heart flips over. He loves when those eyes shine. "Are you going to tell me where we're going yet?"

"No."

"I know it's somewhere warm since you packed my summer clothes." Will grins and pokes him in the side. "Are you really going to make me wait for the details until we land?"

Patrick shrugs.

Will unbuckles and launches a full assault on Patrick,

tickling him, uselessly—since he's not ticklish—and laughing. "Tell me. Tell me now."

Patrick grips his hands and kisses him quiet.

The pilot interrupts what is undoubtedly leading to their induction into the Mile High Club by saying, "Mr. Patterson, Dr. McCloud, I hope you're comfortable in the back. We'll land to refuel at LAX, and then head directly to Kona International on the Big Island of Hawaii. If you need us, just give us a shout through the intercom buttons."

Patrick sighs as Will whoops. There goes that surprise.

"Hawaii?" Will wriggles down to his knees and insinuates himself between Patrick's. "I've never been."

"I know."

"I've always wanted to go!" Will's grin makes all the effort he's put in worthwhile.

"I know."

"Aw, you love me."

Patrick squirms in his chair, somehow embarrassed even though he's wearing the wedding ring that proves his ridiculously gross love for and utter devotion to Will. "Of course I love you," he gripes. "You're all—" he waves at Will's face. "Like that."

Will grins like the sun. "I love you too. What's the plan? Where are we staying?"

"The Big Island for six days and then Kauai for four."

"That's amazing!"

Patrick taps at his left leg and frowns out the window, worry that Will might end up disappointed after all welling up. "I did a lot of research. It'll be romantic. Jenny double-checked me and said you'll like it."

Will laughs. "Dr. McCloud, I do believe you deserve a midflight blow job."

Patrick's dick agrees, and he shifts in his seat. "I'm glad you're happy."

"Oh, I'm happy," Will says, working open Patrick's belt buckle and shifting open his shorts. "And I'm going to show you just how happy."

HOURS LATER, WILL watches Patrick sleep. He's adorable with his head tilted at an awkward angle, his mouth hanging open, and drool sliding from the corner of his lips. Will huffs a laugh. He's still got it pretty bad if a drooling, awkward, rumpled Patrick counts as adorable. And yet his heart feels like it's made of Play-Doh—squishable and soft—as he studies Patrick's sleeping face.

He leans back in his seat and turns toward the window. They've been flying through an endless swath of blue above and blue below ever since they left the coast of California. He wishes he could sleep, but his mind keeps racing.

Thoughts of the ten days ahead, wondering where they'll be staying, and excitement at the fact that Patrick's phone is turned off—*off!*—and will stay that way for their entire trip are all tempered by the return of the usual clinging, tugging guilt.

He remembers when he and Ryan first started dating, how they'd planned to go to Hawaii together one day. Even though he hasn't kept up with Ryan at all since their acrimonious and nasty breakup, he knows Ryan never got a chance to go.

And he also knows that's not his fault. More than that, he knows he wouldn't change anything; he wouldn't go back and be with Ryan for anything in the world.

But his chest still hurts to think of the man he'd once loved—sick love or not—fading away in a hospital bed. To know that the heart he'd listened to on the rare occasions Ryan let him snuggle in close will soon stop beating forever.

A cluster of clouds breaks up the endless blue, and Will studies their shapes, trying to make sense of his feelings.

Patrick deals with death all the time, and Will's not sure how he does it. Because every time Will faces it, he's thrown for a loop. How does someone go from being alive to being dead? It's inconceivable and yet it's the only thing anyone can count on. It's a fact of life.

"Why are you radiating bad juju?" Patrick asks.

Will whips around to find Patrick wiping away his drool. "That's a racist term disrespecting the beliefs of indigenous West African spirituality."

Patrick shrugs. "That doesn't answer why you're

radiating it."

Will can't stop the smile. "I'm just thinking."

"About?"

"About how lucky I am to be going to Hawaii."

Patrick's blue eyes sharpen. "And…?"

"And about how other people aren't so lucky. Some people never get to go to the places they've dreamed of visiting. Some people get sick. Sometimes they die."

Patrick snorts and unbuckles his seat belt, bending to rummage in the cooler of sandwiches and colas at their feet. He comes up with an egg salad sandwich and a Sprite for himself, as well as a PB&J and Coke for Will.

"Why is our romantic getaway inspiring such morbid thoughts?"

Will unwraps the sandwich and saves himself from answering by taking a large bite. Patrick buckles up again and eats his egg salad like he didn't just put away a chicken wrap an hour ago.

Just when Will thinks he's avoided revealing what he knows about Ryan, Patrick finishes his snack, washes it down with the last of his Sprite, and fixes Will with his probing eyes. "So?"

Sighing, Will takes a sip of Coke and shrugs. "It's not a big deal."

"What's the problem? You wanted to go to Cabo? Or Baton Rouge?"

Will laughs.

"You wanted to see the great city of Cincinnati for our honeymoon? You had a hankering for London?

Paris in the springtime? Even though it's still summer?" Patrick's eyes flicker vulnerably. "Did I screw it up?"

"No!" Will grabs Patrick's hand and squeezes. "No. Hawaii is perfect. It's exactly what I'd hoped for when I let myself be even a little bit specific in my fantasies."

"Then what?"

Will wraps up the rest of his sandwich and caps the cola carefully. He clears his throat. "Well, Caitlin told me something before she left town and I can't shake it out of my head."

"Caitlin," Patrick says slowly.

"Yeah. She said Hartley Kills Enemy was in town recently."

Patrick's lips purse. "I see."

"And then she told me the rest."

Patrick keeps his gaze on Will but doesn't say anything.

"I'm not angry at you," Will says reassuringly.

Patrick's brows drop low. "Why would you be?"

"Because you didn't tell me?"

"Why would I tell you?" Patrick throws up his hands. "It'd just make you sad and, look, I was right. Shocker." He shakes his head, wadding up the egg salad wrapper and tossing it into the cooler. He takes Will's half-eaten sandwich and puts it back too.

"I *am* sad. I wish I didn't know so I wouldn't have to think about it." Will's gut tightens. "Does that make me a bad person?"

"No. There's nothing you can do to help him."

"I could take care of his hospital bills at least. So he doesn't have to worry about that."

Patrick waves that away. "I called the hospital he's staying in when I first heard about it on *The Hurting Times*. His care is covered."

"How?"

Patrick raises a brow. "I have this thing called a salary and I'm allowed to do what I want with it."

"I know. I just…really? You did that? For *him*? You don't even like him."

"I like *you* and I knew you wouldn't want him getting less than quality care." Patrick shrugs. "It's handled. Now you don't have to worry about that."

Will's throat grows tight. "Why are you so sweet?"

Patrick slings his arm around Will, dragging him into an awkward, seat belt-hampered hug. "Stop asking stupid questions. And for Pete's sake, I'm not sweet. Ugh."

Will laughs wetly and sighs against Patrick's warm throat. "I love you."

"I know," Patrick barks. "We've covered all this. I love you. You love me. We're on our honeymoon." He gags a little like the whole thing is gross. "Let's not belabor it."

Will unbuckles his seat belt and kisses Patrick hard. When he's breathless, he presses his forehead to Patrick's and whispers, "No, but listen. I really, *really* love you."

"I really, *really* know," Patrick whispers back.

"Mr. Patterson, Dr. McCloud, we'll be landing at

Kona International in approximately twenty-five minutes. We caught a nice tail wind and we're arriving a little early." The captain's voice speaks over Will's reflexive, teary laughter.

"Buckle up," Patrick says. "Safety first."

With a grin of anticipation, Will does. They gaze out the window together, looking for the black lava rock and green of the Big Island of Hawaii to come into view.

Chapter Seven

"THE RUNWAY WAS built on an 1801 lava flow from Hua—" Patrick tilts his head. "Hualālai. Did I pronounce that right?"

"Beats me." Will grins, standing by the sculpture of three beautiful hula dancers in the middle of the open-air, tropical-style airport. Their two bags each are at their feet, and they're waiting on the rental car guy. Will takes the time to admire the sun, the blue skies, the palm trees, and his husband.

Patrick's wearing shades, and he's rolled up the short sleeves of his foam-green shirt to show off even more of his freckled arms. His leg hair gleams reddish in the sunlight, exposed by his khaki shorts. He's also wearing flip-flops, which has Will's stomach doing all kinds of strange things he doesn't understand.

Seeing the arch of Patrick's foot in the tropical sunlight shouldn't be so sexy, and yet it is. In Healing, his husband only wears boots, leather dress shoes, or running shoes. The flip-flops almost make him seem like a different person.

Until he talks.

"Hualālai is a shield volcano. Made almost entirely of lava flow." He harrumphs and scrolls further down the page he's reading on his cell phone.

"Is this information from an app?"

"Wikipedia," Patrick says, frowning. "I'd never accept it as a source for anything of importance, but it'll serve for tourism purposes."

Will snorts softly as Patrick continues to explain the historical significance of the airport they've landed at. "Kona is the only entirely outdoor international airport in the world," he says, looking up and adjusting his sunglasses. "Which would be more impressive if the only flights that made them 'international' weren't flights from Canada. Oh, wait. Japan as well. I stand corrected."

Beads of sweat pop up on Patrick's forehead, and a breeze ruffles his curly, auburn hair, glowing coppery in the bright sun. He nods, and a smile loosens the edges of his mouth as he looks around. "I like it."

"Me too." Will hitches his murse higher on his shoulder and adjusts the flower lei over the collar of his pale-yellow shirt. Patrick had bought the flowers for him as soon as they reached the gift shop. His linen shorts are cool in the breeze, though they're very crumpled from the long plane ride. So much for fashion.

"The flowers are good, right?" Patrick asks.

Apparently Jenny had told Patrick buying a lei when they disembarked would be romantic and Will would like it. For some reason Patrick takes Jenny's advice on romance very seriously, and no amount of saying, "You don't need to," was going to dissuade him. So Will had followed, bemused, as Patrick had marched to the closest gift shop and chosen a white and purple lei for him and a yellow one for himself.

Will lifts the lei to his nose and takes a sniff. And heck if it *isn't* romantic, and darn if he *doesn't* like it. Sometimes Jenny is right. "It's good," he agrees, sniffing the spicy flowers again. "Thank you."

Patrick's chuffed expression makes his heart sing, and Will nudges him with his shoulder. "I like yours too."

The yellow flowers of Patrick's lei shiver in the breeze and pick up gold highlights in his hair. Mimicking Will, he sniffs it and shrugs. "It's okay." Then he goes back to reading from his phone, muttering facts under his breath and turning around as if placing the information in physical space.

Will takes in the busy, open airport. "I wonder what happens to the luggage when it rains."

"It gets wet," Patrick answers.

"Huh. I guess it must."

"There he is." Patrick nods toward a dark, squat man approaching them with a sign reading MCCLOUD. "By the way, this part was *my* idea. Not Jenny's." His grin is sharp and excited. Will follows at his heels, curious and eager to see what Patrick's cooked up.

Will's mouth falls open when the man leads them to a burgundy Porsche 911 Carrera with the top down. "Wow," he breathes as the man hands Patrick the keys and says he'll meet them here at the airport to pick the car up before they leave for Kauai.

After the man walks away, Will wheels around to Patrick, a big smile splitting his face. "You rented this?"

"I figured why not? We never get to drive anything like this in Healing. Snow tires and plenty of room for your siblings being the operative words there." He breaks out a wry grin. "Surprised?"

"You can say that. It's awesome."

Patrick lifts his nose in the air haughtily. "Sometimes I think you forget that aside from being the most brilliant doctor in the country, I'm also the coolest man on the planet."

"And the humblest," Will says, putting their bags in the cache between the seats and the back. His heart feels like a balloon—rising, rising rising—and he grips the side of the car so he doesn't float away.

"I'm driving." Patrick hops in and adjusts the seat.

"Of course you are." Will climbs in next to him and puts on his seat belt.

The Hawaiian sun is warm and bright, and it showers them with golden rays. Will waves his hand like royalty and orders, "Drive on, Dr. McCloud."

PATRICK LIKES THE way the sun lights up the golden hair on Will's exposed forearms and how the wind feels racing through his hair. He likes the purring of the

Porsche as it whips down the road next to the ocean. Black lava fields extend toward the mountain in the distance. He even likes the way the air smells. Salty, fresh, and sun baked.

This giddy feeling of blood pumping through his body is called excitement. He's experienced the sensation outside of the OR a few times since he's been married to Will, and he likes it now too. All in all, he's pleased.

A honeymoon is clearly a fantastic idea after all. Who knew?

"We should text everyone and let them all know we've landed safely," Will says, reaching into his murse for his phone.

"No." Patrick adjusts his sunglasses. "Absolutely not."

Will hesitates with his phone in his hand. "But they'll worry."

"We're on a total electronics and social media black-out, remember?"

It's not like it's easy for him either. He's agreed to give up control of his patients for ten whole days without even being available for a consult. Plus he's not going to look at *The Hurting Times,* and that's a real sacrifice for his gossip-loving self.

But even one little slip on the texting front and they could have a Molinaro/Patterson crisis to contend with just when they're supposed to be getting away.

"When they don't hear on the news about a plane crashing into the Pacific, they'll know we made it just fine."

Putting his phone back in his murse without sending the reassuring texts, Will teases, "What will you do for entertainment without *The Hurting Times?* Read medical journals like you do at bedtime?"

"No. I bought a vampire romance Jenny told me about." The sea breeze must have some magical properties, because Patrick swears his shoulders are relaxing with each breath. "It's a series. If I like the first one, I'll get the rest on my Kindle."

Will cracks up, his head tilting back, exposing his handsome throat.

Patrick grins. "What? You think your husband doesn't read fiction?"

"A vampire romance?" His brown eyes twinkle. "Are you kidding me?"

"Nope. I like trashy books to go with my trashy TV shows and trashy gossip."

"That makes sense, I guess." Will gestures toward the bags in the back. "Well, I brought *A Little Life* by Hanya Yanagihara."

"Never heard of it."

"It's supposed to be the next great gay novel."

"Oh, death and misery."

"Maybe, but I read online that a lot of gay men think it's definitely *not* for a variety of reasons. So I'm going to read it and find out for myself."

"Good plan."

They fall into a comfortable silence as they whip past

palm trees and approach a small, cramped-looking town. The black, hard miles of lava fields all around remind Patrick of the sometimes ruthless land of the reservation out beyond Healing. The resemblance doesn't stop there, either.

The town itself has that "everyone must know everyone else" quality that is now all too familiar. Healing doesn't have thick heat beneath a gentle breeze, though, or tropical foliage, or black lava rock, or swarms of tourists.

Tourists are something Healing will never have to worry about.

"Look," Will says as they pass out of the town and onto the highway that leads to the resort. "Graffiti."

Stark white rocks decorate the wide black lava fields, spelling out names, declaring loves and alliances.

Aloha!
Joe wuz here
Terry + Rhonda 4-Ever

"I wonder where they find the white rocks?" Will asks as the graffiti passes out of sight around a bend.

"The white sand beaches." Patrick has read up about the various beaches in Hawaii, the dangers of riptides and sharks, and decided before he left Healing that the risks seemed negligible enough to relax and enjoy their trip.

Will's eyes greedily suck in the horizon. For someone

who's wealthier than God, he's traveled very little in his life. Not that Patrick's been big on travel either. They're both obsessed with their work and, in Will's case, his family has demanded his attention over the years.

Maybe it really is a good thing they're taking this break. It's about time Will saw more than the plains of South Dakota.

"White sand beaches?" Will finally asks, snapping back from wherever he's drifted, blissed out on the sunlight and new sights.

"There are three kinds of beaches here on the Big Island," Patrick spouts. He read about this the prior night when he couldn't sleep for thinking about all the upcoming hours spent high in the air in the jet. "Green sand, black sand, and white sand."

"Green? How? Why?"

"A mineral, olivine, is part of the volcanic material around the beach. It's denser than the other volcanic sand and so it isn't swept out to sea. It leaves a green cast on the beach."

"I want to see them all."

Patrick nods. "We can do that."

As they reach the resort area, the vegetation changes from thick but sporadic wads of green plants and colorful flowers to groomed and carefully chosen trees, bushes, and groundcover.

"This looks nice," Will says, eyes going wide. He leans forward, the wind sweeping his hair back and ruffling his shirt.

"What did you expect? I'm not honeymooning with you in a roadside motel." Patrick frowns and grips the wheel tighter.

"I know. But, look—" he points at the resort rising before them. The buildings are all freshly painted and the tower, where some of the nicer rooms reside, looks grand outlined against the blue sky. "It's really nice."

"It's not the nicest place on the island, actually. I chose it because of the art collection more than the luxury. Though it is luxurious. Don't worry."

"What kind of art collection?" Will asks as they pull up to valet parking.

"Asian and Hawaiian art and antiquities. An impressive collection on permanent display. If we're going to travel, we should get some culture. Two birds. One stone."

Patrick shuts off the car and allows the valet to take the key. He's tempted to threaten the guy with a lawsuit if he so much as breathes wrong on the car while parking it, but Will seems to sense what he's about to say, grabs him by the arm, and pulls him toward the open-air lobby.

Apparently, in Hawaii they like everything to be outside.

"Wow." Will's hand relaxes on Patrick's arm and he grins, peering around the place. The canopied ceiling is peach and so are the few walls. Otherwise, the breeze flows in from all directions along with the scent of the ocean.

Pergolas with flowering vines line the walkways leading off from the lobby area.

"It's so big, and everything's open. I can't help but keep wondering what happens when it rains?"

"Same thing as at the airport. It gets wet."

A deep voice from behind them interjects, "The rain usually comes at an angle that doesn't penetrate the lobby deeply. And if it does, everything dries very quickly in the sun. Are you Dr. McCloud and Mr. Patterson? I'm Arvin Jones."

The short man's dark eyes twinkle in his rugged face. His peach Hawaiian-patterned shirt and beige slacks are loose and airy, like all the other employees Patrick can see, and the nametag on the left side of his chest declares him a personal concierge. "We've prepared your suite and I'm eager to escort you there whenever you're ready."

"Don't we need to check in?" Will asks.

"It's all been taken care of in advance," Arvin says, motioning toward the opposite side of the lobby. Great, peach-colored steps lead down to where a mahogany boat that looks like it could carry eight people rests on a narrow man-made waterway. Patrick knows from looking at the website that the waterway winds through-out the resort as the main means of transportation aside from walking.

"Your ride awaits. Our boat will take you to your room and your bags will join you by underground conveyer. If that's all right with you?"

"Sure," Will agrees.

Patrick nearly declines, preferring to keep his bags close, but Will takes his arm and follows Arvin toward the boat. "Look," he whispers. "Koi."

Fat fish the size of cats, swim through the water—gold, red, orange, and white flashing by.

Patrick climbs into the boat, which is on a runner like a Disneyland ride, and sits. Arvin joins them, rattling off information about the resort while they motor slowly toward their room. Will listens avidly, twisting and turning in his seat as he peers around at all the resort has to offer.

Patrick watches Will instead. He's seen the videos on YouTube and the photos online. He knows what everything looks like and what they can do here. All he cares about is Will's reaction.

And it's perfect.

His brown eyes shine happily, his beautiful mouth is spread wide in a smile, and his grip on Patrick's hand is warm and vibrant.

"The sea-water lagoon is great for snorkeling. You can see many varieties of fish, sea turtles, and get some exercise at the same time. There are multiple pools across the resort. You'll find those on the map. The spa is open for treatments from seven in the morning until seven at night. The various dolphin adventures are popular. You can swim with the dolphins in our pool or arrange to go out on one of our chartered boats to look at them at sea." Arvin waves at numerous coral, peach, or pink buildings as they float by. "Oh, and I believe you're booked for a day by the ocean in one of our meditation beds. Sometimes, if you're lucky, you can see whales from there."

"I can't believe you," Will says when the concierge finally breaks off to converse briefly with the tall, handsome boat driver about their destination.

"Why?"

"This place has everything. It's amazing."

You're amazing, Patrick thinks, but he doesn't say. He tries to keep some dignity in the face of his all-consuming love even now that they're married. He's not ashamed of his feelings, but he doesn't think he needs to vomit them out constantly just because they exist.

Will glances to the concierge and boat driver for an instant, then lets out a huff of happiness before leaning in for a kiss. His tongue is slippery and soft, and his lips sweet and gentle. It doesn't last long, but it's enough.

Patrick takes hold of his chin and thumbs the cleft. "So you're happy?"

"Happy? I'm ecstatic."

"Good." He kisses Will's mouth again. "Welcome to our honeymoon, puddin'-pop."

Chapter Eight

THEIR SUITE IS at the top of a building called Lagoon Tower. There are astounding ocean views through wide windows on one side and a balcony that looks out over the dolphins' pool on the other. From there, they can see the dolphins playing together, the blue water splashing and rippling as they jump.

Their bedroom opens out to the ocean as well, with a small private balcony. They can't see any other rooms from where they are, and except for a path that follows the line of the beach, no one can see their private balcony either.

Will stares out at the water. The ocean breeze drifts in, salty and fresh. He takes a long, deep breath, and a lump forms in his throat. As he lets out his breath, he bites his lip. Surely he's not going to cry? But he might. The thickness in his throat tightens, and he wipes at his eyes.

With the wind in his hair, Will lets the breeze from the glistening, blue ocean calm him. His shoulders relax, his heartbeat slows, and he releases a long, overdue sigh.

South Dakota is half a world away.

He's here, by the side of the Pacific, breathing new air. The sun seeps into him like a drug, pulling him into a heavy calm. The lump in his throat dissipates, and he relaxes his hold on the responsibilities that eat him alive back home.

"Thanks," Patrick says to Arvin back in the living room of the suite. A bellboy has left their bags by the big, fluffy couch positioned across from a giant TV screen. Patrick's voice bounces gently to Will through the open doorways. "We've got it from here."

Then Arvin, who's escorted them all the way and proceeded to show them all the amenities of the room itself, including the Jacuzzi tub and steam sauna, bids Patrick goodbye. Will closes his eyes against the bright sun, blue-green ocean, and lush green plants, and he waits in anticipation. His nipples rise against his T-shirt despite the sunny heat soaking into his skin. He knows Patrick well enough to guess what comes next on their honeymoon.

A smile lifts his lips.

"Alone at last," Patrick says from right behind him. His breath tingles on Will's neck and Will shivers. "So what will we do now, I wonder? With all this free time?"

Turning, Will slings his arms around Patrick's neck and brings him in for a heated kiss. Patrick responds as enthusiastically as ever, gripping Will's hips and tugging him forward, grinding their pelvises together. The ocean breeze rushes over them, and the scent of Patrick's sweat mixes with the salt deliciously.

Tugging at Patrick's shirt with eager fingers, Will moans, "C'mon. Let's shower and then get this honeymoon started."

Between kisses, Patrick doesn't hesitate to get Will's shirt off too. "I thought we already got a jump on the sexing part while we were on the plane."

"Not the same as having you in me."

"Mmm," Patrick murmurs as he licks down Will's neck, giving him goosebumps. "I like the sound of that."

After the shower, they return to the room damp and aroused. The bed is a California King, wider than necessary, but fun to roll around naked on. Once Will's monitor is disconnected again and placed on the bedside table, they kiss and stroke, laughing as they traverse the bed, messing up the perfect white comforter and sheets. They wrestle for position, and Will gives in when Patrick playfully slaps his ass.

"I have a present for you," Patrick says.

"A present?" Will pants, achingly hard, and beyond ready for them to move past making out and get on to full on fucking. He reaches for Patrick's dick and strokes it roughly. "It better be this right here."

"It's a little bit of that and a little bit of…hold on." Patrick gets up, strolls naked as daylight into the living room, and returns with one of their bags. His cock is mouth-wateringly gorgeous, like always.

Will admires its long, hard length pointing straight up from his sandy-auburn bush of pubic hair. He chews on his lip, wanting to touch and lick it, but Patrick's got his "man on a mission" face on, so he knows he'll have to wait.

Patrick tosses the bag on the bed and pulls out a black box with a silver ribbon on it. "Open it."

Will's cock throbs with his heartbeat as he takes the gift from Patrick's hands and removes the ribbon to lift the lid. "I… What is it? How does it work?"

He takes out a flexible, penis-shaped sheath. It's almost like a very thick condom, except it has a knot near the bottom, and a flat end like a butt-plug. But in the middle of the flat part is a hole, wide and long enough to accommodate a hard dick.

"I plan to fuck you a lot this week," Patrick says, gripping Will's hip possessively. "And to avoid a painful trip down memory lane—" Will flashes back to the night they got married in Vegas and the painful morning after. His asshole had been swollen and tender for a few days. "I found this." He holds the toy up and then slips it onto a dildo he's also pulled from the bag.

Now Will can see how it works.

"That goes inside me and then you…fuck it?"

"I fuck *you*. But, yes. I'll put my dick in the hole here. The sheath prevents too much friction for you, and it's lined inside with ridges to increase sensation for me."

"Oh, wow."

"Exactly. And this knot here," Patrick fingers it gently, "helps hold it in. Not to mention it'll nail your prostate. When I thrust, the knot will massage your gland a lot more firmly than my dick alone."

Will swallows, his cock flexing and a drop of pre-come surging to wet the head.

"The thickness of the sheath adds about half an inch of girth." Patrick points at the walls of the toy. "A whole new sensation."

"Wow," Will whispers again.

Patrick grins. "I've reduced you to 'wows.' It's not even in yet. Perfect."

Will scoots back on the bed and lifts his legs. He's already nonverbal, Patrick's right. Besides, he knows Patrick will love his wanton display.

"That's my puddin'-pop," Patrick says with a sharp grin. "Such a sweet, slutty hole you've got for me there."

Will licks his index finger and swirls it around his asshole, teasing himself open as Patrick grabs lube from the bag. Watching, Patrick pumps his own cock before climbing back onto the bed between Will's legs.

"Mmm, let me kiss you first," he whispers, shoving Will's legs back farther and then diving in to claim Will's hole with his mouth.

Will whimpers, clutching his nipples and pinching hard. The sweet, wet sensation of Patrick's lips and tongue against his asshole breaks him out in shivers, and the ocean breeze from the open balcony door caresses his hard cock. He twists his nipples harder, grounding himself in the sensation, moaning as Patrick licks him inside and out.

"That's right," Patrick murmurs, kissing Will's ass cheek before ducking back down to suck another kiss to his hole. "Squirm on my face."

Will groans as Patrick's tongue penetrates him again. He squeezes his nipples hard, and his hips jerk reflexively, balls drawing up tight. A trail of slick precome stripes where his cock rests heavy and hard against his stomach.

Patrick sits up, his mouth red and wet, his eyes dilated with lust. His wiry muscles ripple and flex with each breath, and Will reaches for him, pulling him down for a filthy, open-mouthed kiss.

He tastes himself on Patrick's tongue, and he mewls quietly when Patrick nips his lower lip. Their cocks jam against each other, rubbing like hard velvet up against perfect sensation.

Patrick's back muscles tremble and shift under Will's palms, and when he sits back on his heels, he grabs the dildo-impaled toy. "Hold your legs apart."

Will does as he's told. The fan above the bed swirls gently, the ocean breeze drifting in from the open balcony doors. He shivers and aches, his cock thudding against his stomach, his asshole flexing in anticipation. Sunlight cuts across the bed, and he squints his eyes closed, a smile breaking across his face, as Patrick lubes first the toy, then Will's asshole, and finally his own cock.

"Here we go." Patrick slips the head of the toy against Will. The dildo is still inside the toy, providing the solidity needed to penetrate Will's tight anus. Patrick pushes gently, and Will breathes, bears down, and twists his hips wantonly as the toy slides in. Until the knot bumps up against his rim.

He moans, his asshole tensing against the unexpected thickness.

"That's it," Patrick encourages. "Take it. You know how. Open up."

Will swivels his hips, sucks in a deep breath, lets it out, and bears down hard. The knot stretches his asshole tight. Fresh sweat breaks out on his forehead and he groans. Patrick adds a push and a twist, and Will gasps as the toy pops through. Pain, sharp and hot, rides him for a few harsh breaths, but he waits it out, his cock still aching and eager for more.

Opening his eyes, he holds his legs up and apart, gazing down to where Patrick kneels between them. His thighs are already quivery and weak with lust, and they shake against his palms.

Patrick bites his lip and stares avidly at where the toy is lodged in Will's ass. "Ready?" he whispers.

"Yeah," Will rasps.

Patrick nods and then slowly withdraws the dildo from the sheath, leaving Will open—but not in the rough, unforgiving way of a butt plug. No, he's softly open, the sheath warming inside him, and it feels good, kind of slutty. Like anyone could walk up and push inside. Like Patrick could use him over and over and he'd be ready and able to take it. His cock pulses and precome puddles against his treasure trail.

"Wow," he whispers again. He grips his ass and the sheath flexes with the movement.

Patrick squirts some lube up inside the toy, but Will

doesn't feel the cold like he normally would. He squirms as Patrick fingers him with the toy in, rubbing and pressing against the sides, and pushing the knot against his prostate.

"Can you feel everything?"

"Yes," Will murmurs.

"Perfect."

Patrick kisses Will's calves before raising them to his shoulders and leaning in to thrust. As he slides into the sheath, the extra girth makes Will hunch up and growl. He squirms his hips, reaching down to pull Patrick farther in. "Oh, that's…oh…"

Patrick's eyes squeeze tight and he huffs out a tender sound.

The toy has softened and warmed now. It doesn't feel foreign any longer, just a lot thicker than Patrick usually feels inside him. And the knot presses right against his prostate so that every thrust sends a shock of bliss jolting through his body. "Ohhhh, wow."

"Yeah," Patrick says gruffly, opening his bright blue eyes. Sunlight glints red and gold in his auburn hair. "Squeeze around me."

Will does and Patrick shivers all over. "Good?"

"Too good." Patrick grips Will's hips hard. "This will be a fast fuck, puddin'-pop. But there'll be more where this came from later."

"I'm going to hold you to that."

Will shifts his hips up, catching Patrick's thrusts greedily. They fuck hard and fast, the bed rattling the wall, pleasure bursting in spangles behind Will's closed eyes. Patrick's breath huffs against his neck, hot and humid, and the skin between them grows slick with sweat. Patrick pinches Will's nipples as he fucks him, his fingers finding the perfect pressure to make Will twist and cry out softly.

The fuck isn't as fast as Patrick promised. Instead, Will finds time stretching as his pleasure is prolonged. His thighs and hips quiver, his asshole spasms and releases, but the sheath holds him open and friction free. The stimulation on his prostate is intense and grows steadily hotter and more penetrating, like the sun that warms the room. Like the scent of the flowers drifting in, filling him with tropical heat and want. He whimpers and arches, seeking the stroke that will take him over into mindless bliss.

Patrick kisses him and the world dissolves to the sweat between them, the wordless grunts rising around them, and the rocking, rutting, gathering glory between his legs.

Will's hand goes down to his cock, alternately gripping his balls to stave off orgasm and then fucking wildly into his loose fist. "That's it," he murmurs. "There. Just like that."

Patrick obeys, fucking him like the waves on the beach, hard and steady, relentless, until Will cries out and convulses, his ass spasming helplessly around Patrick and the sheath. His come shoots from his cock and splatters his chest and stomach. His balls tighten and another spurt of jizz rockets across his hot cheek.

"Yes," Patrick hisses. "That's it. Come for me."

Will arches his back, and sensation like shards of hot pleasure rake him as Patrick continues to nail his oversensitive prostate. "It's too much," he whispers. "It's…I'm, oh, here….yes!"

His asshole convulses again as the wave-like anal orgasm he's only experienced after long bouts of rough fucking rises up and washes over him. He jerks hard on the bed while Patrick praises him. His body wracks with pleasure. He shouts into his fist, trying to stifle the noise, and he grabs Patrick around the waist, holding on as another hit of pleasure rocks him.

Will loves this toy.

Patrick keeps right on fucking him, driving that knot into his prostate, and Will digs his nails into Patrick's back, roars, and nearly levitates off the bed, as another spurt of come shoots from his dick.

Patrick pulls out—red and flushed from chest to cheeks—and quickly runs his hand over his cock twice before shooting all over Will's dick, pubes, and stomach.

"Yeah," Patrick groans, head back, prominent Adam's apple on display.

Will pulls Patrick down, smearing the come between them, and shudders hard. "Love you," he whispers.

"Mmm," Patrick agrees, nuzzling Will's neck.

Will basks in the pleasure for a few minutes, enjoying the scent of sweat, their come, and the salt air. But then Patrick pulls away, grabs Will's murse from the chair by the bed, and Will sighs as the usual stick-test routine begins.

When they're both sure Will's BG is good, Patrick slowly removes the sheath from Will's ass.

"I'm going to leave the best review for this on *The Hurting Times* product recommendation thread," Patrick says, as they walk naked together toward the bathroom to clean up.

"I will kill you if you do." Will takes Patrick's hand and squeezes hard.

Patrick smirks. "I'll do it anonymously. No one will have to know."

"Because so many people in Healing are eager to share anal sex toy recommendations?" Will says with a raised brow.

Patrick tosses the sheath in the sink and turns on the hot water. "You know as well as I do the kinky things people get up to in that town. Anal sex isn't even close to the most interesting thing cooking."

"We're on a full electronics break," Will reminds him.

"I wasn't going to type it up now. Though I do think I'll make some written notes. I'd hate any of the best details to be left out. Like how the internal ribbing felt on my dick when you squeezed your ass around it." He grins. "Don't get me wrong. Your ass alone is perfection. It's hard to improve on that, but they came close."

Will rolls his eyes and decides to fight Patrick over it when he's actually typing up the review. They wash each other and Patrick cleans the sheath before they head back into the bedroom, damp and naked.

The glimmer of an early Hawaiian afternoon shines on their skin. The breeze from the open balcony drifts in and washes away the lingering scent of their union. They curl up against each other and drift lightly to sleep.

Will dreams of swimming with a pack of dolphins that turn slowly, one by one, into members of his family. He tries to swim away from them, but they keep catching up. He kicks harder and harder, but the dolphins gain ground. He can't get away. He knows it deep inside. When he looks over, the dolphin beside him has Ryan's face. Tears burn behind his eyes.

Will wakes to his first Hawaiian sunset with a knot of guilt in his stomach, jet lag clouding his mind, and Patrick snoring happily by his side.

Chapter Nine

"VIRGIN STRAWBERRY DAIQUIRI," Will orders, his sunglasses glinting.

Patrick loves the way Will's exposed skin and hair shine in the tropical light. It reminds him of when they first got married and he thought Will was "glowy," which is still a description that is all kinds of ugh, but is also all kinds of true. And Patrick adores Will so much that he's happy to indulge in such romantic ridiculousness inside his own head.

"Make sure it's a virgin daiquiri," Patrick chimes in, adjusting his own floppy sunhat and slathering more sunscreen on his bare shoulders. "And I'll have a lemonade."

"Will do, sir," replies the handsome young pool boy who, moments earlier, had emerged from the small café to take their order. He scampers off, his pert young ass looking adorable in his khaki uniform shorts.

"He plays for our team," Patrick says.

"Yeah," Will agrees.

They're sitting poolside as evening descends on their first full day in Hawaii. They spent it having sex, ordering room service, reading and admiring their view, as well as sleeping at all the wrong times, as jet lag caught up to them. But now they're awake and enjoying themselves. It's still warm enough to wear their bathing suits, though the breeze is cooler now. Many of the employees have donned cardigans and some of the other tourists have as well. They must not be from South Dakota where fifty-nine degrees is swimming-pool weather.

"I bet he rakes in the tips from married older men who want him to meet up somewhere private once the wifey is asleep."

"You always think the worst of people," Will says softly.

"I think the *people* of people," Patrick corrects. "Human beings are messy and awful most of the time, but that's life."

"Such a misanthrope."

"Hardly. *You're* the misanthrope."

Will laughs. "I'm the do-gooder, remember? Hello? I love people and try to help them."

"You love the idea that people can be perfect. That they're *fixable*. That you can pour money and time into someone and they'll become a better friend, lover, or person. I, by contrast, accept that people are usually awful and always will be. I only want to fix their broken brains, not their minds. But that doesn't mean I think they don't deserve love and acceptance."

"Just not yours."

Patrick shrugs. "They don't need mine."

The pool boy returns with their drinks and Patrick catches him glance down at Will's stomach, at the visible transmitter and infusion site, but the man says nothing, giving Will a charming smile as he hands over the daiquiri.

Patrick takes the lemonade offered by the pool boy and the tab. He signs it to the room along with a tip, and the pool boy scampers off to help an elderly lady whose walker is stuck in the pebbles by the sidewalk leading down to the saltwater lagoon.

Patrick says, "I'm choosy, but it doesn't mean I think the people I *don't* love—which is mostly everyone—don't deserve someone else's affections."

Patrick's feeling lazy and is in no mood to move, but he doesn't mind winding Will up to get their adrenaline pumping so they can screw again.

But Will just sips his drink and smiles to himself, gazing calmly at the blue of the pool. Patrick wonders what's going on in his head. He's ready for their usual squabble to ensue. The one where Will flushes prettily and tells him what a terrible man he is, and Patrick disputes that assessment, and then they have a small fight before they fuck and make up.

As Patrick watches, the sky turns the color of an orange. Most other tourists have left to get ready for dinner or grab good seats for the nightly luau, which includes an impressive show called The Legends of Hawaii complete with dancing and fireworks.

"You're not perfect," Will finally says, sipping his

drink again. "And I don't want you to be. I love you all messy and weird like you are. And you're wrong that I want everyone to be perfect. I just want everyone to be happy."

"Never going to happen."

"Maybe not." Will reaches out to tweak Patrick's floppy hat. "But we're happy. So who knows? If we can do it, surely other people can."

Patrick straightens the hat again.

Will laughs. "The sun is setting. I think it's safe to take that off now."

Patrick frowns. "I burn easily." He glances around the pool area at the lack of umbrellas. "This place is made for dreamboats with dark skin, not people like me."

Will relaxes in his seat and muses, "Connor always burns too. The curse of the redhead."

Patrick shrugs and removes the hat anyway. "I have it better than he does. At least I tan beneath the freckles."

Will leans over and lifts his sunglasses, examining Patrick's shoulders and chest. "I've never seen you with this many before."

"I excel at them like I excel at everything else I do."

Will laughs and then turns his bright sunshine smile up to the sky. "I'm happy, Patrick. I'm glad we're here."

"I am too."

"You don't miss brains?"

"Not yet. Maybe tomorrow. But with any luck some

idiot kid will slip on the pool deck and I can perform emergency miracle surgery right here on the sandy sidewalk."

"Ha."

Patrick smiles. His lemonade is fresh and sweet enough to rot his teeth. Just the way he likes it. "We'll have to explore down there tomorrow." He nods toward the lagoon.

"Sounds good to me."

"What do you want to do tonight?"

"Walk the path down by the ocean? Maybe look at some of that art you came to see?"

"And then we'll have sex again."

Will chokes a little on his daiquiri before laughing. "Yeah, okay."

"Perfect." Patrick stretches back in the pool chair, enjoying having his feet up.

He realizes that, until Will brought it up, he hasn't thought about surgery or brains all day. It's a surprise because those are two of his favorite things to think about. But he can't say he's been bored since they landed in Hawaii. He's content even.

Which is strange.

He's used to having the low-grade aggravation of constant Patterson-Molinaro drama in his life. If he shrugs off the lingering tension in his muscles, and gets laid one more time, he might just be what is known as *relaxed*. It's an interesting feeling. And kind of cool.

"This has been a good day," he declares. "Yesterday

was good too. Even with flying in a tin can at forty-one thousand feet."

Will doesn't answer. He just smiles and tilts his head back, pushing the sunglasses on top of his head and peering at the sunset's colors. He sips his daiquiri and they rest together in silence.

Patrick reaches out and takes Will's fingers. Then they wait like that together until the sun goes down, leaving the sky the color of a bruise.

As they stroll along the path up from the ocean after their walk, early stars twinkling overhead and the lush foliage surrounding them, Will hums a new pop hit under his breath that Patrick doesn't entirely hate. A small sea turtle crosses their path, shiny with water and determined to crawl into the long grass opposite, and they pause to watch it go.

A hand lands on Will's shoulder, jerking him around.

"Hey!" Patrick shouts, fingers clenching into fists and his heart racing as he wheels around to confront whoever's dared touch Will.

"Guglielmo! It *is* you!"

The use of Will's given name and the dimple creasing the cheeks of the ridiculously handsome dark-haired man in front of them is all Patrick needs to understand that the peaceful, romantic honeymoon they've been enjoying has collided with a brick wall known as Tony Molinaro.

Will's insane, mafioso, biological father.

Will gapes. "Dad?"

Chapter Ten

T ONY WEARS A red, blue, green, and yellow floral Hawaiian shirt that billows in the breeze from the ocean. His trim body is hidden beneath the voluminous fabric, but his fit legs extend from the tailored khaki shorts he wears. His dark eyes are gorgeous and deep, and his smile is a crack of white across his tan face.

Patrick hates that his father-in-law is damn hot, though he credits the man's genes with Will's pelt of chest hair that he loves so much.

Tony draws Will into a hug and pounds his back. "Son! It's been too long!"

"Only four months, actually." Will speaks it into the wind and Patrick's not sure Tony hears.

"I've missed you!"

It's been closer to five months since Tony last swept through Healing, boned Kimberly in all kinds of inappropriate places, set *The Hurting Times* on fire with gossip, then left as quickly as he'd arrived.

At least he hadn't impregnated the woman. The only reason Patrick's sure of that, given how reckless they both are with their sex lives and their family planning, is that Kimberly is petite enough that she'd be showing by now.

"I've missed you." Tony clasps Will close again. "How's your mother? Is she here?"

"She's fine. No, she's in Healing."

Tony keeps an arm around Will's shoulder but turns his head this way and that, searching, like they're hiding Kimberly in the flowering bushes by the walkway. "But why isn't she here? And the children too?"

Will's mouth opens and closes spasmodically.

"Why *should* she be here?" Patrick snaps. "She has a life."

That's a pretty generous way to put what Kimberly has, but he's not in the mood to have his honeymoon spoiled by Will's family, and the Molinaro side least of all. Call him petty, but he still has his panties in a twist over the way Tony threatened to cut off his fingers if he hurt Will, and the "come to the Dark Side" conversations he's been subjected to more than once since their marriage haven't improved relations much.

Tony smiles warmly at Patrick. "Ah, my favorite son-in-law hasn't lost his bite. I like him, Guglielmo. I really do."

"I know. You tell me all the time."

He leans closer and whispers in Will's ear. "I'd like him more if he came to work for me."

"You can't always get what you want," Patrick said, sticking out his lips like Mick Jagger.

Will smiles tightly, all the easy relaxation of earlier

evaporated, his shoulders drawn up to his ears.

Tony's eyes glint happily. "It's shame really. We'd make a good team. A *lucrative* team and—"

"Dad, what are you doing here?" Will interrupts, ducking out from under Tony's muscled arm.

"Me? Oh, well, I'm…" he glances behind him. "Darling? Where are you? Are you playing hide-and-seek?"

A woman pops out from the bushes, adjusting her flowing halter-top sundress, putting away her very large and obviously recently exposed breasts. She giggles, her long blond hair slipping over her bare, sunburned shoulders as she ties her dress up around her neck again. "Silly Tony! I'm here. I needed to get decent."

Tony waves his hand. "These two wouldn't have cared, darling. They're queer as three-dollar bills." Then he smiles at them like that's a compliment. "And Dr. McCloud's been through medical school. He's seen it all."

The woman laughs again like Tony is actually funny and steps forward with her dress fixed and floating in the breeze.

"Angelica Madison," she says, smiling with glowing white teeth that make Patrick think of his father's dentures. He shudders.

The woman can't be more than twenty-six, just a few years younger than Will. Or maybe she's had so much plastic surgery she just looks quite young in the darkness. Either way, Patrick braces himself for what's coming next because he can feel it, like the chill on the breeze.

It's coming, coming, coming…

Now.

"Oh wait!" She throws her head back and laughs. "I forgot. I'm Angelica Molinaro now." She squeals and holds up her hand. A giant diamond glints on her ring finger in the moonlight.

Will swallows hard next to him, and Patrick reaches out to put a hand on his lower back. "Oh, um…I…" Will blinks rapidly. "Wow."

"The operative word yet again," Patrick mutters. He puts out his hand to take Angelica's. "Nice rock. Good luck on the rest of it."

Tony leans over and whispers, "Now that divorce is a Molinaro birth right once more, I can have a little more fun with my romances. You know what I'm saying?" He nudges Patrick suggestively. "Nothing quite like a spontaneous wedding to get the heart pumping. I know you understand."

Will lifts a hand and tries to speak, but no words come out.

"We're big fans of impromptu weddings," Patrick agrees. "Makes for fantastic wedding nights."

"You're telling me." Tony slides his arm around the giggling Angelica's waist. "Almost as good as some of the best nights I've had with Will's mother."

"I can't," Will says and turns on his heel, walking away.

Angelica laughs like her new husband isn't standing on the sidewalk of a resort in Hawaii discussing their marriage like it's a game.

"He's always been uptight," Tony says fondly as he watches Will retreat.

Patrick jerks his thumb over his shoulder. "Yes, well, as Will goes, so goes my nation." He's proud of himself for slipping in a *Buffy* reference his criminally ridiculous father-in-law will never get.

"Oh!" Angelica cries, pointing at him. "That makes you Oz, right?"

Patrick narrows his eyes at her, says nothing, and turns away, following Will toward the path back to their suite.

"Oh, and don't tell your mother about this!" Tony calls out to their retreating backs. "She never likes it when I get married!"

Will shakes his head and speeds up so that Patrick has to jog to catch him.

"How did *I* come from *them*?" Will asks the sweet night air. "More importantly, *why*?"

Patrick slings his arm around Will's shoulder. "I guess sex is off the table now."

Will closes his eyes and lets Patrick guide him a few steps before sighing and putting his arm around Patrick's lower back. "I don't know. We'll see how I feel."

WILL PANTS IN the afterglow. His asshole is loose and still open with the new toy Patrick had pressed in before he'd set about fucking him like the world was ending. His now-flaccid cock tingles from coming hard again, and his muscles are limp and exhausted.

The swirl of sleep offers to drag him down and out for the night, but Patrick's sticking and testing, and Will flutters his eyes open when Patrick makes a frustrated sound at the result.

"Juice or a frosting tube?" Patrick asks.

"Juice," he mutters and hauls himself up enough to take the cold bottle from Patrick's hand. He sips the tangy orange juice and tries to keep his mind from thinking, tries very hard to just stay with Patrick in the quiet luxury of their hotel suite. But of course it's no use. He groans as the memory of running into his father and his new bride worms its way through the after-bliss.

"We can leave this resort early. Head over to Kauai now," Patrick says, reading the direction of Will's mind. Then he nudges Will's legs apart and eases the toy out, leaving Will's asshole to flex on air as he tightens up again.

"No. I wanted to swim with the dolphins, and spend the day you booked in the seaside meditation bed. And you wanted to see the art."

Patrick goes into the bathroom to wash the toy and his hands. Will continues to contemplate the offer to leave early. But he says nothing, sipping his juice quietly until Patrick returns, drying his hands on a towel. "No," Will says again, determinedly. "We didn't even get to explore the lagoon yet. Let's stay."

After Will finishes his juice, Patrick takes his hand again, sticks and tests, grunts in satisfaction, and then hooks up Will up to his BG monitor. Tossing a pair of boxers at Will, he watches as Will pulls them on, attaches the monitor, and they settle into the giant white-sheeted bed together.

"Do you think he planned this? Just to mess with me?"

"No one but Jenny and I knew we were coming here," Patrick says.

"Jenny wouldn't tell."

"No." Patrick settles down against Will, pillowed against him in his usual way. His sigh glides through Will's chest hair, a ghost of comfort.

"So this is a horrible coincidence."

"Looks like."

Will squeezes his eyes closed. "Did you see her? She's my age."

"He's a dirty dog. But we already knew that."

"But…but…" Will throws his hands up, jostling Patrick. "Why would he marry her?"

"For giggles, apparently." Patrick shrugs, yawns, and settles more firmly against Will's chest. "Why does your father do anything?"

"Money and power."

"And pleasure."

Will stares at the ceiling fan. "What does she see in him?"

"Patrick snorts. "He's hot. Like, smoking hot."

Will wrinkles his nose and sneers. "Ew."

"I'm sorry you can't handle the truth." Patrick sits up and looks Will in the eye. "Your dad's sex on legs. Your uncle isn't half-bad either. You've got good genes, I can't lie." He turns off the lights on the nightstands. The room descends into darkness except for the moon glinting on the ocean visible through the sliding glass door to the balcony.

When Patrick eases back into his spot against his side, Will moans, "Is our honeymoon ruined now?"

"Like I said, we can head to Kauai early. Or go to Maui. We've got money to burn so let's burn it on reckless vacationing. Just say the word."

"No," Will whispers, his voice shaking as a fire lights in his chest. "I'm not going to let him ruin this for me. Not like he's ruined so many other things in my life. This trip is ours and we're not going to let it go. Okay?" He takes hold of Patrick's hand and squeezes. "Promise me."

"Why should we do that? Let's get the hell out of Dodge and save ourselves the grief."

"Because you planned this honeymoon for six months and I won't be denied what you planned for me." Will's chin trembles, but he's determined. "Promise me."

Patrick groans but runs his fingers soothingly through Will's chest hair. "Fine. I promise you can stay here and let your dad run roughshod over our plans."

Will groans and covers his eyes with his elbow. Patrick's right, but he's so sick of letting his family screw up his life. "I could call Nonna. Maybe she'd convince him to leave us in peace? She is his mother, after all."

Patrick laughs. "Ha! Like she's so good at convincing him to stop screwing your mother in the middle of the damn street every few months?"

"It was in the alley behind the tack shop," Will corrects.

"My bad."

Will squeezes Patrick closer. "You're right. It's no use. He does what he wants." Will's monitor beeps and he rolls his eyes. "I was so relaxed earlier. Now I'm stressed and this," he waves at his insulin pump in the dark, "knows it."

"Maui is nice." Patrick sits up and turns on the lights again. He inspects the numbers on Will's pump and frowns. "Jenny was pushing hard for me to book a few days in there."

"I told you. He's not going to win. What's my BG?"

"Well, he might not win, but we're sure to lose." Patrick flicks the lights out again. "It's fine. You're fine. Just a little high, but the pump should compensate."

"Okay." Will knows Patrick hates how stubborn he can be, but this time it's for a good cause. "But we're not going to Maui. Our honeymoon, the one you planned for us, will prevail."

"Fine. Love wins," Patrick agrees, snuggling in for the night.

Will nods and kisses the top of his head. "Always."

Chapter Eleven

B UT IT DOESN'T feel like love is winning the next morning when he and Will wind up sitting across from Angelica and Tony over breakfast in one of the resort's large, peach-colored dining rooms.

"So, I figured why not get married while I'm down here working out this deal for a new casino." Tony smiles winningly, and his handsome hazel eyes gleam in the morning light.

"Mmm," Patrick says around his mouthful of pan-cake-wrapped bacon. He digs in for another bite, partially because he's starving, and the bacon's really good, but also to keep his snarking to a minimum. Will's already unraveling at the seams, he can tell. He doesn't want something he says to be the thing that sends Will into a meltdown.

"Angelica has never been married, so I offered to show her the ropes," Tony says, winking at his bride.

She's as young as Patrick initially thought the night before. Maybe younger. Her teeth and eyes have the shine of youth. And her breasts, with the nipples visible through the light, cream-colored sundress, are perkier than the meringue tips on the banana pudding she's eating. She's a tight young thing, and Tony is a pervert and a half to be tapping that.

Not that Patrick has any right to pass judgment about age differences in love affairs. But he and Will aren't even ten years apart. Tony and Angelica must be close to twenty.

"What do you do for a living, Angelica?" Will asks with a tense smile, clearly trying to keep the conversation from turning into an elaboration on whatever Tony meant by showing the girl the ropes.

"I dance," she says, tossing her blond hair over her shoulder and grinning widely.

Will takes a moment to digest this announcement, rubbing at his golden morning stubble, left unshaven at Patrick's insistence that they head down to breakfast before he keeled over dead from starvation. "Dance. How interesting. Ballet or…modern?"

"Lap."

Will chokes on the water he's sipping. Tony laughs, throwing his head back and exposing his long neck. When Patrick has to talk to him, he grows less and less attractive, but when the man just shuts up and exists, he's downright fine. Hopefully Will is going to age half as well.

Angelica giggles. "I learned from the best stripper on Oahu. Millie the Fierce. Do you know of her? She's amazing. She dances at Hawaii By Night. Have you been?"

"No," Will whispers, taking up his water again and gulping half of it down. His monitor alarms and he looks down at the numbers, frowns, checks his pump, and then focuses on Angelica again. His cheeks flush and sweat shines on his forehead.

"We're gay," Patrick says. "Remember? Papa Molinaro here told you last night. Strip clubs and Millie aren't our jam."

"Oh, but we have some handsome men who dance there too." She smiles widely again, somehow completely innocent of how absurd everything about this conversation is. But such is Patrick's life since he woke up married.

"Oh?" Patrick asks, his interest perking up. "Men, you say? Tell me more."

Will kicks him under the table as Angelica answers, "They're all so handsome! Buff and strong. Slim and trim. We cater to all types at Hawaii by Night!"

"Wait," Will says, pushing his half-eaten breakfast away. "How did you...when did you..." He shakes his head, rubs a hand over his face and tries again. "When did you meet, exactly?"

"Oh, last week." Tony grins. "I flew in to Oahu for a few days before I needed to meet with my contacts regarding the casino deal I'm working on here. I have a small operation going in the nightclubs on Oahu. Just a little pain pill business—" He waggles his brows.

Will shakes his head. "I don't want to hear about that."

Tony shrugs. "While I was checking in on my investment at Hawaii By Night, I met Angelica, and the rest is history." He tweaks one of Angelica's blond locks and she smiles prettily at him.

"Love at first sight?" Patrick snipes.

"Of course not!" Angelica laughs. "He's in love with someone named Kimberly. Duh. I'm just for fun."

Will's face goes pale and he shakes his head. "You're for *fun?* You're a human being! You're for…a lot of things! But you're not 'just for fun'!"

"Oh, but I like it." She cocks her head at Will, her copper-brown eyes shining. "He'll enjoy me and when he's done with me, I'll go away. He'll let me keep this ring." She raises up the honking big diamond taking up half her finger again. "It'll get me enough in pawn to go back to college. Right, Tony?" She takes Tony's hand before she leans forward and whispers confidentially, "It's a mutually *beneficent* thing."

"Beneficial. Mutually beneficial," Patrick can't help but correct.

"That's what I said." She glows. "Tony is the best thing that's ever happened to me."

Will stares at her with wide eyes. Then he turns to his father, holding out his hands like he's seeking some kind of reason in this madness. "So…help me understand. Why get married? Couldn't you just give her money for college and sleep with her?"

"I'm not a prostitute," Angelica says, sniffing delicately. "I'm a wife."

Tony kisses Angelica's cheek and slips an arm around her shoulder.

"But why?" Will begs, ignoring Angelica's valid, in Patrick's opinion, point.

Tony's eyes gleam. "For fun!"

"And strategy," Patrick surmises.

Will glances back and forth between them. "What kind of strategy includes marrying a stripper?"

Patrick's not sure when he figured it out exactly—sometime between his first sip of coffee and now—but, suddenly, it's crystal clear. "The kind of strategy that involves getting your mother all riled up. Somehow he knew we were coming here, despite me only telling Jenny about this, and for some reason, he thought Kimberly would be here as well. I'm not sure how that fits in with his casino and happy pills business, but Kimberly's why he's really here. Isn't it, Tony?"

Tony's brows go up and he leans forward with a sharp grin. "You're my favorite son-in-law. You realize that, don't you?"

"He's your only son-in-law," Will growls.

"Your sister Ellen is getting married before long." Tony rolls his eyes and sighs. "To a loser of a man. No imagination. No fun. Nothing to offer."

Will blinks at him. "Right. My sister Ellen." Then he clarifies for Patrick, "She's one of the half-sisters I've never met."

"Ah."

"Yes, exactly. And why should you meet her?" Tony

asks. "She's dull as dishwater and she's marrying a boring yes-man. He smiles too much." Tony shudders. "I prefer men like Patrick. You understand?"

"No. I don't understand you," Will says. "I'll never understand you. I don't even know where to *start* with how much you confuse me."

Patrick pops a melon ball in his mouth and sits back to wait for the show. Here it comes. In three, two, one…

Will throws his napkin on the table. "You know what? I *do* know where I want to start. *Why* would you think Mom would be on our honeymoon? And *why* would marrying a stripper be strategic if she was? What are you up to, Dad? And why are you here ruining my romantic trip with Patrick?"

"I already told you last night. You mother doesn't like it when I get married."

Will rolls his eyes. "Are you kidding me? So what? This is just an attempt to get her upset so you can…" Will trails off, his eyes narrowing. "Really?"

"The rage sex is always so good." Tony shrugs. He leans over to his wife and whispers, "Not that you're not delightful, darling. But Kimberly brings a certain fire that can't be matched."

"I'd love to meet her," Angelica says. "If she's as beautiful as you say."

"More beautiful than I can describe," Tony says fondly. "Especially when she's angry."

Will scrubs his hands over his face. "Fine. Never mind. I get it. You're a sick bastard."

"Yes, I am," he says proudly. "A sick man with a signed pre-nup and a beautiful woman in my bed. The wrong beautiful woman, but she'll do. For now."

"For fun!" Angelica chirps and winks.

"Okay, well, answer my first question then. Why would Mom be on our honeymoon?" Will picks up his glass of water and drains it.

"I assumed this was a family vacation," Tony says. "Your friend Jenny Burger mentioned your upcoming travel to the man in the coffee shop, the one she sleeps with, and she just happened to talk about this resort specifically. It was pure coincidence that she did so in front of one the men I've had stationed around town to watch out for your mother."

"Spy on her," Patrick says.

"Spy. Protect. It's such a fine line. Regardless, it's your friend Jenny's fault I'm here. She spilled the beans to the man in the coffee shop and those beans got to me just in time to make a detour to Hawaii before I head back to Los Angeles to check on a deal there." Tony frowns. "What is the coffee shop guy's name? It's slipped my mind."

"Jax," Will supplies.

"She better have made up with him," Patrick grumbles.

"No, she didn't. She's sleeping with her ex again," Tony says, eyes wide. "The father of her son? It's all over *The Hurting Times*. The townspeople are taking bets on how long he stays in Healing this time. If he knows what's good for him, it won't be long."

Patrick grits his teeth. Now he itches to check *The Hurting Times* app to make sure Tony's telling the truth. The gossip columns will have the latest, and he can call Jenny to tell her off if she's really giving Tom another go. But his and Will's phones are locked up in the safe in their room.

"Maybe you should call her," Will says.

"No." Patrick shakes his head. "Phone calls are a slippery slope. We'll never be able to place just one."

"Like potato chips," Angelica says wisely, nodding and laughing so that her pert nipples shake.

Will frowns at his empty glass, looks around for a waiter to refill it. Not finding one, he takes Patrick's water instead. Patrick frowns, and just as a suspicion kicks in, the monitor alarms again.

"What's it say?" he asks, leaning close to Will, trying to read the numbers. Another thing he misses about his phone: instant access to Will's BG readings.

Then he smells it. He leans closer to Will to confirm. Yep. Concentrated Band-Aid odor. The specific and intense scent of a big, fat problem.

"C'mon." He stands and grabs Will's arm. "We need to get you back to the room."

Tony frowns. "What's the matter? Is Will okay?"

Will doesn't rise. He darts his eyes between Patrick and his pump. "It's not a big deal. The pump shows the boluses. I'm fine. I'm just thirsty." He reaches for his plate of food and grabs another strip of bacon.

"Let's go," Patrick says again.

"Just let me finish breakfast," Will snaps.

"No, I think now," Patrick tugs on his arm harder. "You're drinking water like you're in the middle of a desert and I smell Band-Aids."

"Oh." Will says, frowning. "Oh."

He actually looks like he's going to argue with Patrick about this, which isn't a surprise since extreme irritability is another sign of oncoming ketoacidosis. He'd probably have noticed that first on a normal day, but, well…Tony.

"Where's your murse?" Patrick asks. He can solve this problem right now with an injection, but, for the first time in forever, Will seems to have left it behind.

"I don't need it. That's what the pump's for," Will growls. "We're on our honeymoon. How romantic is it to carry that thing around everywhere?"

"Unless you think an ER run is romantic, we need to get back to the room."

Tony stands and motions for a waiter to come over. "We need a doctor," he says urgently.

"I *am* a doctor," Patrick hisses at him. "Just come with me, Will. Now."

"Fine." Will throws his napkin down and stands, his cheeks flushed and his eyes gleaming feverishly. "Just stop telling me what to do!"

Patrick takes a deep breath, reminding himself that this childish rage is just the high BG speaking. "Or I can let your dad call the hotel doctor and we can make a big honking drama out of this."

"I'm leaving!" Will stomps away in the direction of their room.

"He's fine," Patrick says to Tony, who makes a move to follow. "He needs to change his infusion site. His pump's leaking insulin. It's not getting into his system."

"We'll come with you, won't we, darling?" he says to Angelica.

"Of course," she says, rising with big eyes. "Anything to help my step-son!"

"No. You'll make things worse." Patrick holds up his hands and glares daggers at them both. "Stay here."

Tony reaches out to grab Patrick's arm as he passes. "Have dinner with us tonight, then."

Patrick rolls his eyes. "Thanks, but we're having room service."

"Surely not with such lovely, romantic views to take in from one of the private dining rooms. Have you even attended a luau yet?"

Patrick barks. "What don't you get about this? It's our honeymoon. We'll do what we want."

"Ours too," Angelica says, smiling again like an oblivious but very pretty sheep.

"Right." Patrick nods at her sharply. "Let's each keep our honeymoons to ourselves. No sharing. Got it? Good."

Tony's eyes take on a strange gleam as Patrick turns away from him. He doesn't have time to figure out why, though, since he has to jog to keep up with Will.

"Gotta pee," Will says when he reaches him on the

walkway. His expression is disoriented as he looks around desperately for a bathroom.

"I bet."

Patrick steers him to the closest one, follows him in, lingers by the urinal and compliments him on his dick size just to be annoying. Will snarls, but as they exit and start toward their rooms again, he says fairly coherently, "I think my infusion site got yanked." His CGM shrieks again and he looks down. "Yeah. No doubt about that."

Patrick puts a hand on his lower back and guides him toward the closest boat dock. "Let's ride back. It'll be a little faster."

"You think?" Will barks.

Patrick swallows back his instinctive response and says, "You're cute when you're going into ketoacidosis."

"I am not."

Patrick laughs under his breath and helps Will onto the boat. "You're right, puddin'-pop. You're not. You're an absolute jerk."

"Now you know what it's like living with you."

"Good burn," Patrick says, calmly. "I've taught you well."

Will glares at him but Patrick just smiles. All they need to do is get to their room and fix Will up, then Patrick will have his sweet do-gooder back and he can return to being the King Jackass in their relationship.

Forty-five minutes later, propped on their suite's sofa with a fresh infusion site supplying Will with insulin and a glass of water in his hands to help flush out the ketones, Will murmurs sheepishly, "I'm sorry I was a jerk."

Patrick shrugs and rubs his feet where they're propped in his lap. "Yeah, well, if you suck my dick, it'll be worth it."

Will laughs, his eyes twinkling. "Oh, yeah?"

"Yeah."

Will drains his glass. "C'mere. Let me suck your dick before I have to take a leak again."

Chuckling, Patrick unzips, scoots across the sofa, and kneels up to straddle Will's chest and fuck into Will's mouth. It doesn't take long because the sight of a flushed Will with his red mouth wrapped around Patrick's dick just never gets old.

He threads his fingers through Will's hair and thrusts deep into his throat, soothing him when he gags. The scratch of Will's stubble on his balls is delicious, and Patrick remembers that he wants to make Will rub his chin against other sensitive places before he shaves it off.

When Will closes his eyes and relaxes his throat, proving himself to be the cock-sucking champion Patrick's long known him to be, it quickly gets to be too much. Patrick backs away slightly as he comes hard, emptying his balls down Will's throat and milking the last drops of spunk from his dick to smear on Will's lips.

"Yep, worth it," he sighs, zipping up as Will licks the excess come from his lips. "Now let's see about you, shall we? I want to get my fingers in that hole of yours. What do you think?"

Will shifts down and unbuttons his shorts. "I think you're the doctor and that you know what's best for me."

Patrick's spent dick twitches. "Oh, yeah? Are you my patient?"

Will nods. "Yes, Dr. McCloud. I'm very sick and need your medical opinion."

Patrick stifles his grin and puts on a serious expression. "Mr. Patterson, your blood glucose is stabilized, but as your doctor I'd be negligent if I didn't ask when you last had your prostate checked."

"It's been hours." Will's brown eyes are wide and innocent.

Patrick tsks. "That'll never do. It's important for good prostate health to have the gland examined regularly. Let me check it now before you leave my office."

Will's cheeks glow and he shoves his shorts down. "Thank you, Dr. McCloud. I do need to have it checked. You're right."

"Oh, I'm always right," Patrick purrs, already planning a very long and involved check-up for his patient. "Now turn over on your stomach and spread your legs for me."

Chapter Twelve

THE BREEZE SHIVERS through his hair as Will climbs out of the Porsche and follows Patrick into the hotel after turning the car back over to the valet. It's been a full day and a half of successfully avoiding Tony Molinaro and his new bride, and he's feeling much improved.

They'd spent the morning exploring the offerings of the salt-water lagoon. But when Patrick spotted Tony and Angelica on a nearby walkway, they'd hightailed it out of the resort to take the car to Waialea, also known as Beach 69, for the day.

They snorkeled and played in the waves for hours. Children and families dotted the beach and splashed all around them. It was chaotic and yet peaceful, the sound of the water and waves drowning out details of other people's conversations, until Will had felt they were alone in the beautiful ocean.

Once they were deliciously tired from the salt water and fresh air, Will spread out to dry off in the sun while Patrick huddled beneath a rented umbrella with his floppy hat, scads of titanium dioxide sunscreen, and read his trashy vampire book. Then they'd made out like teenagers behind a rock outcropping before jumping into the rented Porsche to head back.

As far as Will's concerned, it's been a perfect day. His shoulders are loose, his spirits high, and his skin more tan than ever before. In contrast, Patrick is red, hungry, and grumpy. Despite his best efforts not to burn, he's pink all over and freckles have burst out on his shoulders, arms, and chest like hidden treasure surfacing. Will loves them, but Patrick finds them annoying. At the moment, tired and hungry as he is, Patrick seems to find *everything* annoying.

Will doesn't care. He thinks Patrick's adorable this way and, on the drive home, he gave him a kiss on his wrist for every grouchy comment.

"That idiot valet better not scratch that perfect piece of machinery," Patrick grumbles as he watches the young man pull away in the Porsche.

Will grabs his arm and kisses his wrist again.

"Stop that," Patrick mutters. "You're getting me all slobbery."

Will licks his wrist this time.

Patrick rolls up the sleeve of his T-shirt emblazoned with a picture of half a glass of water and the words *"Half air. Half water. Technically, the glass is always full."* He pokes at his red shoulder. "I better book an appointment with an dermatological oncologist when I get home to get a jump on the incipient skin cancer treatment."

"You're barely red."

"All burns are—"

"Bad burns. I know." Will kisses Patrick's wrist again.

Eyes flit their way in disgust, a subtle homophobia he's almost forgotten about in the strangely safe enclave that is Healing, South Dakota. For the most part, the resort in Hawaii has been a safe haven as well, but there's plenty of anti-gay sentiment in the world, and lots of their fellow tourists have brought it along with them.

"Slather me with aloe and then kiss my asshole for an hour and I'll be happy again," Patrick mutters. A woman standing too near gasps, and Patrick glares at her. "Mind your own business."

"Don't worry," Will says to her as they pass. He giggles, feeling drunk from the hours in the sun and water. "I like kissing his asshole." He doesn't know what's possessed him. That sort of comment is more Patrick's speed, but he laughs even harder at her shocked face.

"Someone needs to loosen up, huh?" he says as they push deeper into the main lobby, heading toward the boat back to their suite. "She'd probably like her asshole kissed too."

"Mmm," Patrick says, noncommittally. "I'm hungry. Let's order room service. Plates and plates of room service."

Will smiles. Patrick's in the food zone now and nothing will distract him from it, not even the joy of scandalizing the other tourists.

"*William Patterson*! Where on earth have you been?"

Patrick jolts to a stop before Will does and they slam together. Will blinks rapidly, his skin racing with goosebumps at the shrill sound of his mother's voice.

No. It's impossible. It can't be.

Slowly, they turn to find Kimberly standing a few feet away in the lobby, her hands on her hips, sunglasses slung low on her nose so she can glare at them, and her silk sundress dancing in the constant Hawaiian breeze.

"Mom?" Will swallows hard. "What are you doing here?"

Patrick pinches the bridge of his nose, whispering, "You've *got* to be kidding me."

"What am I doing here? I'll tell you what I'm doing here," she says, striding toward him on three-inch heels. She points a perfectly manicured nail into his chest. "You, young man. You're the reason I'm here. You didn't call me!"

Will's heart squeezes and releases. "Because I'm on my honeymoon?" he asks, somehow unsure of that given everything that's transpired in the last few days. "And I'm fine?" He swallows thickly. "Is there something wrong? Is everyone okay?" Uncle Kevin? Is he—"

Kimberly dismisses his concern with a fast wave of her hand. "Everyone's fine at home. But you? You are *not* fine! I heard about your trip to the ER!"

"What? I didn't...wait. What?" Will sputters and runs his hands through his hair. "What is *going on*, Mom?"

"Tony's going on," Patrick interrupts before Kimberly can answer. His eyes narrow on her. "Let me guess, Tony called and told you Will had some trouble with his pump the other day and insinuated he was in the hospital."

Kimberly tosses her hair over his shoulder. "I tried to call. I didn't get through to either of you on your cell phones."

"I'm assuming you called the hospitals, though?" Patrick asks.

"You know as well as I do they don't give out patient information to anyone these days. Not even mothers."

Patrick rolls his eyes. "Bull crap. They told you he wasn't a patient there, but you came anyway."

"You could have called the front desk. Left a message," Will says, joining in on Patrick's outrage. "Since you clearly know where we're staying somehow." His eyes fill with tears. "Why would you come here? To do…what? Crash our honeymoon? Are you *crashing our honeymoon*, Mom?"

"I am most certainly *not* crashing your honeymoon." Kimberly lifts her chin, but there's some uncertainty to her voice. "I'm here to make sure you're safe."

"And?" Patrick prompts.

She glares at him and turns back to Will. "And to see your father. He seems to have gotten into some kind of scrape with a woman and needs help getting out of it." She smooths her skirt down and looks away.

Patrick groans. "Kauai. Tomorrow. We're leaving for

Kauai tomorrow. End of discussion."

"No!" Will nearly shouts. His heart is in his throat. "I want to do the meditation bed by the ocean tomorrow. I want to take the art tour you planned."

Patrick glares at Kimberly. "You see what you've done? You've made him angry. Way to go."

"Oh, you think *he's* angry? You don't know angry until your diabetic son doesn't answer his phone," Kimberly says, pointing her pink talon at Patrick now. "I'd think you, as a doctor, would understand that."

"I'd think you, as a semi-intelligent adult, would stop racing across the world to throw your legs open for Tony Molinaro, but it looks like we'd both be wrong."

Will huffs out a half-sob, half-sigh, and rubs his hand over his face. "How'd I ever think I could have a normal honeymoon? What crack was I smoking?"

"Molinaro-Patterson family crack," Patrick says, glaring at Kimberly as he runs a soothing hand down Will's back. "If I could locate the supply I'd destroy it all."

Kimberly pops a hip and removes her sunglasses. She studies Will closely like she'll see the lies written on his skin. Will almost feels all the old ones he's never confessed to her drawing up to the surface under her scrutiny. "Are you telling me you weren't in the ER yesterday after going into ketoacidosis?"

Will takes a slow breath, trying to stay calm. "What I'm telling you, Mom, is that even if I was in the hospital—which I wasn't—I'm a grown man, and I don't have to call my mommy to come flying across the world to hold my hand. I have a husband for that."

"Would your husband call me if you were dying?" Kimberly pins Patrick with hard eyes. "I think not."

"I wasn't dying! I wasn't even in the hospital!" Will waves his hands in the air, fury and frustration gathering in a lump in his throat. "And of course he'd call you if I was dying! I can't believe you don't trust him."

"Actually, I probably wouldn't," Patrick says, calmly. "She's a bad risk for you when you're sick. I'd avoid calling her for as long I possible."

"Not now." Will glares at him, shaking his head. "Don't be so honest right now."

"Fine." Patrick mimes zipping his lips.

Turning back to his mother, Will sighs. "I can't believe you flew all the way here over this."

"Of course I did! Any mother would!" Her attention goes back to Patrick. "Wouldn't Dinah come if you were in the hospital? Of course she'd come."

"Dinah would make sure I was actually there first."

"And how would she do that when you don't answer your phone?"

"She's a smart lady. She'd figure it out."

The tension between Kimberly and Patrick sizzles, and Will steps between them before it gets any further out of hand. "I'm sorry you were scared for me, Mom. I really am. But I was fine. The whole time."

"It's not just about you, William. You can't just keep your phone turned off like this. What if there was an emergency? What if Caitlin, Olivia, or Connor needed you?"

Patrick blows a raspberry at her guilt trip.

Will closes his eyes and summons patience. "If there was a true emergency, Jenny would know about it, and she knows where we are." Will rubs his mother's shoulder. "She'd have contacted the hotel and they'd have made sure we got the message. Do you understand?"

"You better. Because it's ridiculous to interfere like this," Patrick gestures at her sharply. "And it's exactly what we were trying to avoid."

Kimberly's eyes fill with tears. "Well, when you're a mother and you hear your son is in the hospital possibly dying—"

"He said I was dying?" Will can't believe his father would take the farce that far just to get Kimberly to Hawaii for a too horrible to imagine fuck fest.

"No, but you might have been!" she exclaims. "You know what happened the last time you went to the hospital!"

"That was a few ER trips ago, actually." Will gently squeezes her shoulder and peers into her eyes, trying to pass his seriousness and sincerity through to her. "I haven't come close to dying in a long time."

"Don't remind me how often you end up in the hospital, young man! It does *not* make me feel better!" She blinks tears from her blue eyes and digs in her purse for a tissue.

"Speaking of hospitals," Patrick says, rubbing his temples before giving her a half-smile. "How's Kevin's dumb head? Good as new I hope?"

"He's taking care of the children. He's *fine*." She wipes at her nose. "He just has to stay off the horses for a while. That's all."

"Good to hear." Patrick nods, considering. "I guess I'll have to trust Dr. Lerma's opinion." Though it is obvious to Will that he wants to check Kevin over again himself.

"Look, this is Dad's fault, okay?" Will says, returning his focus to his mom. "He wanted you here and he got what he wanted."

"Where is he?" she asks, looking around hopefully. She straightens her dress and runs a hand over her hair. "I've tried to text him since I landed but he hasn't answered."

"He's probably enjoying his new bride," Patrick says. "In a bush. Or on the beach. Somewhere public if possible. The way he likes it best."

Will pleads, "Patrick, don't."

Kimberly stares at Patrick, opens her mouth, and shuts it. And then her eyes don't just fill with tears—they spill over.

"Mom?" Will asks, pulling her into his arms. "Hey, don't cry. I'm fine. I'm sorry I yelled at you—"

"I'm not sorry," Patrick says, rolling his eyes.

Will ignores him and when his mother doesn't stop crying, he steers her toward a bench beneath a pergola strewn with pink and yellow flowers on a vine. It's out of the way of the main lobby and less public. They've made enough of a spectacle.

"I'm not crying about you," Kimberly says, reaching into her purse to pull out a tissue.

"You're not?"

"No. Of course not." She waves dismissively at him. "You're fine."

Will grinds his teeth as he takes a seat beside his mother. Patrick's stomach growls and Will sighs. It's only a matter of time before Patrick gets truly hangry, if he isn't already. And Will needs dinner too. For his health.

"How can I help you, Mom?" he asks, hoping to cut to the chase, but most conversations with his parents are like labyrinths. He can get in, but he can't get out.

"Did you say Tony is married?" Kimberly asks, her gaze swerving back to Patrick.

"As married as ketchups in a diner," Patrick confirms.

Her lips twist slightly, but she sits up straighter. Her voice is tight when she asks, "To whom?"

"Angelica Madison." Patrick raises a brow. "Stripper extraordinaire. Lovely girl. She's *fun*."

"Patrick…" Will warns again. The Hawaiian breeze washes over them along with the scent of jasmine.

Kimberly closes her eyes and shakes her head. "I'm such a fool."

"Tell me more," Patrick says.

Will shoots Patrick a silencing glare until he puts up

his hands in surrender.

Kimberly seems to have taken Patrick's snark seriously. "When he said he was in a scrape with some woman, I thought he was trying to make me jealous so that I'd come down here to 'save' him. I didn't think…" She sniffles again. "You mean he's actually…he married her?"

"For fun," Patrick says again. But gently this time, like he's trying to be sweet and reassuring. Will's stomach flutters and his heart softens. Underneath his gruff exterior, Patrick is a healer and he'll always try to ease anyone's suffering. Even someone he doesn't like very much.

"It's just a fling." Will pushes a hank of his mother's hair behind her ear. "He's just trying to bait you."

"And it worked," Patrick points out.

Kimberly pats at her eyes with the tissue. "Did my mascara run?"

"No," Will whispers.

"Good." She straightens her shoulders, puts her chin up, and the tears are replaced by a glare. "I want to look my best when I give him a piece of my mind."

"And your ass."

"Patrick!" Will snaps, his relaxed mood from earlier dissolved in the glare of the late-afternoon sun and his mother's red eyes. "Mom, calm down and just…"

"No, I need to find him," Kimberly says, standing up and smoothing her dress again. "Now that I know you're safe, I'll help your father disentangle himself from the clutches of this gold digger. Even if he doesn't deserve my help."

"Diamond digger." Patrick spreads his hands wide. "She's got a huge tooting diamond she plans to sell."

"To fund her return to college," Will confirms, rising and taking his mother's hand.

Kimberly frowns. "Good lord, if the man wanted me to come down here for a tropical fling, you'd think he'd just call. He knows that's all it'd take." She rolls her eyes. "Why make up something about you being in the hospital? Why marry some..." She waves her hand around. A parrot squawks in a nearby cage.

"Some stripper?" Patrick offers.

Will watches as a butterfly flies close by and lands in one of the flowering bushes next to the pergola. "I guess he thinks this is more—"

"Fun," Patrick says again.

"Yeah," Will rubs a hand over his face and his monitor alarm goes off. He glances down at the numbers. "Low." He slings his murse down off his shoulder and takes out a small tube of frosting and opens it, squirting the sickly sweet contents into his mouth and closing his eyes.

Patrick raises a brow at Kimberly. "Stop stressing him out."

"I'm not," she says irritably. "You both stressed *me* out. Well, you and his father."

"Then go find his father." Patrick takes Will's hand and pulls him up from the bench. "We're on our honeymoon and you're not welcome to be part of it."

Kimberly gasps, but Patrick doesn't wait to start up another argument with her. Will doesn't fight him as he leads the way toward the boat dock to catch a ride back to their rooms.

Rolling the sweetness of the frosting around in his mouth, Will sighs again. He doesn't even look back over his shoulder to make sure she's okay. His mother can fend for herself. He's done pretending his entire family isn't legitimately insane.

At least until after they've eaten dinner.

And after he's spent some time kissing Patrick's asshole.

Then maybe he'll be willing to think about his family and their dramas again. But he doubts it. He's on his honeymoon with Patrick and he's going to dedicate every single bit of his brainpower to enjoying it.

Even if his family is determined to make that really, really hard. Or impossible.

Chapter Thirteen

"Do you want to see the volcanoes?" Patrick asks the next morning as they walk around the resort, finally taking the independent art tour Patrick arranged to see the outdoor collection without what he called "an annoying and probably idiotic docent."

"Mmm, I don't know." Will tilts his head to examine a statue from Japan. It looks much the same as the last four statues they've seen, but he's sure there's some important difference that Patrick will illuminate by reading aloud from the collection's guidebook.

He ponders it. "I'd rather stay around the resort for the most part. Maybe tomorrow we can hit a black sand beach like we talked about, but…" Will reaches out and touches Patrick's tender nose. "You're already burned. We should stay in the shade."

Patrick adjusts his floppy hat and sunglasses, nodding. "Fine by me. Who needs volcanoes? Things have been explosive enough around here."

"Sexy explosive or angry explosive?" Will already knows the answer.

"Both." Patrick frowns and flips the guidebook

closed. He glances down at his watch. "Our appointment for the seaside meditation bed is soon. We might as well walk that way."

"Did you see everything you wanted to look at? With the art, I mean?"

Patrick nods. "And now I want to look at you naked."

Will glances around and lowers his voice even more. "But I thought the meditation beds are outside?"

Patrick arches a brow. "They are. Come on."

As they walk the paths of the resort, heading toward the small building where they check in for their appointment with the meditation beds, Patrick snags Will's hand. Will squeezes his long, fine fingers.

"Do you remember when we first agreed to stay married?" Patrick asks, his thumb stroking over Will's knuckles, his eyes narrowing on the tall man approaching on the path who does a too-obvious double take at their latched hands.

"When I came to see you at Dinah's?"

"Yes."

"I don't think I'll ever forget it. I was scared you wouldn't take me back."

Patrick snorts. "Yes, well, I did. Lucky you."

"And lucky you."

"Right. I've been thinking."

"Yeah?"

"Don't you think we should get a move on with the other thing we agreed on then?"

"What other thing?"

"The part about making a family." Patrick clears his throat, his thumb going still on Will's knuckles and his other hand rubbing self-consciously at his face.

Will's jaw drops. "You want to talk about starting a family?"

"We've been married a few years. I'm not getting any younger."

"Wow."

"Wow, what? Have you changed your mind?" Patrick's Adam's apple bobs as he swallows convulsively. "Because I haven't changed mine."

Will pulls him toward a bench beneath a vine-wrapped pergola and they sit, hands still clasped. "Of course I haven't changed my mind. I just thought I'd be the one trying to convince you."

"Okay. Good. For a minute, I thought…" He shrugs and straightens. "We should start when we get back."

"Start talking or…?"

"Start the process. Just start."

"We can't just start. There's a lot to consider. I mean, I haven't changed my mind, but I didn't think you'd want to do this now."

"Why not?" Patrick frowns. "I've been waiting for you to say you're ready. It's what you want. What we both want." He nods decisively. "Let's just do it."

"It's not like it'll be easy for us. There are a lot of hoops we'll have to jump through. Choices to make. Things to decide."

"Fine. We'll do those things."

"We haven't even discussed if we're going the surrogacy or adoption route."

"Details."

"Important details." Will studies Patrick's face, taking in the sharp edge of his jaw and the stubborn set of his mouth. "Why now? I mean, here we are trying to have a honeymoon and the family we *already* have is making that close to impossible. I'd think all of this would make you wary of bringing anyone else into this mess, much less a baby."

"True. That would be the logical conclusion. It would make the most sense to keep any other human being, especially innocent ones, far away from the crap show that is the Patterson-Molinaro clan, but…" He trails off for the second time in just a few minutes, a lack of precision that speaks of deep feelings, or confusion between his logical mind and his emotions. It makes Will's heart thump.

"But?" Will prompts. The fresh freckles on Patrick's nose stand out, and Will wants to trace them with his finger.

"But you're a Patterson-Molinaro and you're my favorite human on earth, and those siblings of yours don't suck, and neither do babies."

"You *love* babies." Will waits for the inevitable denial of this incontrovertible fact, but it doesn't come.

Patrick shifts uncomfortably.

"What? Tell me."

"As annoying as it is to admit, I do love babies. And lately I keep thinking about how much I'd love *your* baby."

"Our baby."

"Yes, I'd love it a heck of a lot."

Will's stomach wriggles giddily. "I would too."

"We'd protect it from the craziness, and if we couldn't, then we'd teach him or her to endure it. Promote character development."

Will laughs. "Okay, well, I can't believe I'm the one suggesting we put the brakes on this for a little while longer. But, how about this? When we get home, we can start a list of discussion points. Things we need to decide before we can really begin."

Patrick squeezes Will's hand again. "You're not backing out?"

"Absolutely not. But there's so much to decide. If we use a surrogate, we need to decide if it'll be someone we know or someone we hire. If we adopt, we need to choose local or international. I've dealt with some LGBT adoption stuff, grants to help offset the costs mainly, through Good Works. It's not easy stuff."

"I just want to know we're going to do it. After all, when I married you, I was promised a baby." Patrick's smile turns into a smirk.

"I remember it was more me trying to convince you than any kind of promise."

"Tomato, to-mah-to. Let's go. We only have a few minutes before our appointment. I hate being late."

Will's heart aches fondly as they walk, hands still together, to the check-in. His mind swirls with thoughts of making a family with Patrick: what their baby will look like, how they'll parent together, and how to keep their child sane in a world of Patterson-Molinaro madness.

The meditation beds are placed far apart on the rock outcrops lining the resort's ocean front property. They're white curtained and canopied with the only open side facing the sea. And even the open side has a privacy screen that can be dropped if they're worried about people on passing boats or jet skis seeing what they're up to.

Will strips down to his underwear, leaving his monitor attached, and folds his clothes in a neat stack in the cubby at the head of the bed. "Let's leave the family talk behind," he says. "We're still on our honeymoon, after all." Then he stretches out on the warm, soft sheets, smiling invitingly.

Patrick strips completely, of course, shameless as ever about his body, and drops onto the bed next to him, his white ass up. He waves at the water shimmering out to the horizon. The family discussion seems as good as dropped. "Romantic, right?"

Will smiles and rolls to his side, admiring his husband's lazy sprawl. Some people might hear arrogance in Patrick's voice, but Will hears the underlying vulnerability too: *Is this okay? Am I doing it right?*

"Very romantic. I'm glad you planned this for us."

Patrick shoots Will his sharp, sexy grin, and flips

onto his back. "Another thing I excel at: vacation planning." Then he frowns. "But next time I'm thinking we'll go somewhere truly isolated. The mountains of Tibet maybe. Or a long stay in a yurt in Mongolia. Your family wouldn't have the skill set to find us there. Except Eleanora. She could manage it."

Will sighs and watches a spray of water flash in the air as a wave shatters on the lava rocks below their bed. "Tony could pay someone to manage it."

"True. Speaking of your parents, they looked cozy this morning." Patrick waggles his eyebrows. "Who knew your mother was flexible in more ways than one?"

"Shh, let's pretend they aren't here."

"Deal," Patrick agrees.

Will breathes out, low and long, and tries to forget that they'd glimpsed Kimberly, Tony, and Angelica breakfasting together that morning. He and Patrick had darted out of the restaurant before they were spotted to grab protein smoothies by the pool instead.

Still, it'd taken an hour for Will to shake the image of the three of them laughing and casually touching in ways he doesn't want to contemplate too hard. It's one thing to know his mother and father can't keep their hands off each other. It's another to think about a third party added to the mix.

"I'm worried about Jenny," Patrick says after a few minutes of silence spent listening to birdcalls, the flapping of the wind in the curtains around them, and the crash of the ocean waves.

"Yeah? Do you want to call her?"

Patrick shakes his head, a frown etching his brow, his eyes focused on the ocean. "Her asshole ex isn't going to stay. And this time she's got Dylan involved in it too."

"And Dylan loves Jax," Will murmurs, sympathy for Jenny's son welling inside. He knows all too well what it's like to get attached to someone his mother is dating, only to have that all fall apart when his biological dad comes swirling back into town.

"Yeah."

They both consider this a moment.

"Well, she's an idiot." Patrick rubs his eyes quickly, like he's wiping away the worry before rolling onto his side to face Will. His cock is flaccid, but as it flops on his leg, it shifts and swells.

"What have you got there?" Will whispers, reaching out to run his forefinger gently down the growing length of Patrick's dick.

"Like I've told you, my childhood nickname was Snake."

Will laughs, rolling his eyes.

"Go on. You show me yours since I'm showing mine."

Will glances around like the white curtains are suddenly see-through, but then he shoves his underwear down and detaches his pump and wires, stuffing everything in the cubby, satisfied with the readings and certain he can play for an hour or so without concern.

He stretches out on his back. Blood rushes south

when Patrick reaches out to take hold of him, and he hardens the last few centimeters in Patrick's skilled hand.

"I have a nice tight hole this looks like it could plug," Patrick says seriously, examining Will's cock like it's something he's considering buying.

"Maybe you should show me."

Patrick grins, flips around, and moves quickly to straddle Will's face, bending low to breathe hot, sticky air over Will's cock while Will slides his hands up to massage Patrick's taut ass.

The saltwater breeze rushes over them again, and Will shivers, maneuvering one of the fluffy pillows beneath his neck so he doesn't have to strain so hard to reach Patrick's asshole.

"It looks like it'll do the trick," Patrick mutters, licking the head of Will's cock.

Spreading Patrick's ass cheeks apart, Will glimpses his tight anus. He pushes them together again to hide it, a teasing game of peek-a-boo with the part of Patrick he most wants to kiss right now. But he makes himself wait, and makes Patrick wait, until hot, wet, heat engulfs his dick.

Will squirms as Patrick slides down, down, down and buries Will's cock in his throat.

"Show off," Will grunts. He knows he's good at giving head. Patrick praises his efforts all the time. But Patrick's the deep-throat champion of the world as far as Will can tell.

Patrick doesn't say anything, just starts bobbing up

and down, a sexy, wet gargling sound coming from his throat as he works. Will quivers, the breeze from the ocean teasing his nipples and flitting in his hair.

"Mmmngh." Will spreads his thighs, hoping Patrick will play with his hole, and sets his attention on Patrick's pleasure.

Musky and tender, Patrick's asshole twitches against Will's tongue as he screws determinedly past the tight ring of muscle. Patrick shoves his ass back, pulling off Will's cock to gasp for air before diving back down again.

With wet heat on his groin and Patrick's sweet hole under his lips, Will wallows in the scents and sounds of their lovemaking. The water below laps, breaks, and crashes against the land.

After bringing Will close to climax twice, Patrick pulls away, sits up, and grabs the small backpack he brought from the room. The tube of lube is nearly gone after the week they've had, but there's enough to swipe a gob over his open, saliva-wet asshole, and then dribble some over the head of Will's cock.

Patrick tops more often than not—it's the way they both prefer. But Will loves that when Patrick wants to be fucked he just *goes for it.*

He's no different now.

Straddling Will's hips, he reaches down and guides Will inside, his head dropping back, mouth hanging open, and a groan of pain mixed with pleasure rolling out of his throat.

Will moans too. As his cock sinks into Patrick's tight heat, Will admires his husband. He runs his hands up Patrick's thighs, over his lean stomach, and up to his sparse chest hair.

The filtered sunlight glistens over Patrick's body, shining gold and red in his auburn hair. The wind keeps his skin cool to the touch, and Will's not sure if it's the breeze or his light touch that raises goosebumps along Patrick's flesh.

"C'mere," he whispers, reaching up to tangle his fingers into Patrick's hair and guide him down into a kiss.

The slap of their skin together, the wet exploration of their tongues, and the tight heat of where they're joined melds with the sea air and cries of gulls in an easy, lazy fuck, until Will rolls Patrick onto his back and drives into him hard enough to guarantee Patrick sees stars.

Patrick grunts, his fingers scrambling against Will's sweaty back, sliding down to grip handfuls of ass cheek. "Make me come."

Will buries his face in Patrick's neck, licking the salt from his skin and kissing behind his ear. Patrick whimpers and wriggles a hand between them, taking hold of his hard cock and jerking himself rapidly.

Will doesn't slow his thrusts as Patrick's spare, trim form tightens beneath him, and his breathing grows strained with effort. He plunges his cock into the hotness of Patrick's body again and again, watching avidly as Patrick's eyes shift in and out of focus.

Patrick's freckles stand out on his red cheeks. His muscles go taut, and his eyes fly open wide. He stares up at Will with a fragile vulnerability that cuts through to Will's heart every time, and then he groans, come spurting between them as he comes apart.

Wrapping his arms tightly around Patrick's trembling body, Will pumps hard until his own climax sweeps over him. He comes deep inside Patrick, heart overflowing with tenderness and love.

PATRICK SLOWLY RISES off Will's cock and flops onto his back next to him, the wind making him shiver as the sweat is wicked from his body and into the Hawaiian air. His thighs shake, and his asshole twinges from the rough use.

"One thing I always say about you, Will Patterson." He reaches out to join their hands. "You're a great fuck."

Glistening with sweat and come, Will pants out, "You 'always say' that about me, huh? To who?"

"Anyone who'll listen."

Will laughs, his eyes scrunching up adorably. Patrick frowns at his own mental description. He's always extra-mushy after he's been fucked. It's a thing.

"I should be horrified because that's probably true," Will murmurs.

"It *is* true! All of it." Patrick praises Will's sex skills every chance he gets. After all, Will spent far too many years being shamed for one of his greatest gifts. "You're amazing in bed. The best I've ever had."

"You know I'm always glad to hear it," Will teases, poking Patrick in the ribs until he barks in laughter. The curtains flap around them. "But you don't have to tell everyone!"

Moving away from Will's finger, Patrick disagrees. "Yes, I do. It keeps the doctor chasers away."

"Oh yeah? Doctor chasers?"

"Every hospital has some and being gay doesn't make me exempt."

Will's brows lift curiously. "And what do these doctor chasers say when informed of my out-of-this-world bedroom skills?"

"They usually offer to show me how they can outshine you," Patrick grumbles. "They really don't know how to take no for an answer. Not until I make them cry, anyway."

"You'd do that even if they weren't offering to suck your dick."

"If they'd concentrate on their jobs, there'd be less tears all around." He squeezes Will's hand and shrugs. "I can't help it if I'm hot as hell, but they really need to learn their place."

"Nurses," Will says, shaking his head with mirth.

"Speaking of nurses, your uncle thinks I'm banging Varun."

Will's eyebrows climb to his hairline. "Why does he think that?"

"Because I said some things to him about Varun being pretty. I was just trying to hook the poor guy up. When's the last time Kevin got laid? A million years, I bet."

"Let's not talk about my uncle having sex."

"We're talking about him *not* having sex. Keep up, puddin'-pop."

"Wrong. We're not talking about him and sex at all. Okay? We're in Hawaii, naked by the side of the ocean. Let's leave my uncle fully clothed in Healing where he belongs."

"With the kids. While your mom and dad have a threesome with a stripper on our honeymoon. Oh, the mid-Western sweetness of it all."

"It's a fairy tale, this life we lead." Will chuckles, his eyes shining brightly. "We really are an old married couple if this is our pillow talk."

"Now you're the wrong one. Old married couples' pillow talk is stuff like, 'Get butter at the store,' and 'Don't forget to put on your adult diaper.'" He grins, a bubble of amusement in his chest. "Oh, the many joys we have to look forward to."

"Sexy."

"You know it."

"Do you really want to grow old with me?" Will asks.

"Nah. I married you for your hot young ass and when it's wrinkled I'm outta here."

Will's lips twist up in a small smile. "There was a time when hearing something like that from the man I loved would have terrified me. I'd have thought he meant it. But with you, I know you're not going anywhere. Ever. You love me."

"It's really gross, and I don't recommend the emotion to anyone with sense enough to avoid falling into it, but, yes. I do."

Will motions at the streaks of come drying all over his stomach. "How do we clean this up before it dries in my pubic hair?"

"Like this." Patrick leans over and licks along Will's softly-defined abs, cleaning up the mess with his tongue. Will's cock slowly rises again, his body shifting against the sheets and his legs spreading wide in invitation. Patrick sucks on two fingers and then slides them inside, laughing quietly when Will's hips buck up and his skin flushes with renewed need.

"So how long do we have this bed?" Will gasps, squirming as Patrick nails his prostate.

"All afternoon."

"Want to sixty-nine for a while?"

Patrick grins. "Why not? I'm all for sucking and fucking the rest of the day away."

"Me too." Will writhes on Patrick's fingers and cries out softly.

The breeze and surf blends with the sounds and scents of their lovemaking until the sun starts to go down. Patrick's heart is light and his body trembles with exhaustion by the time he shoots one last time into Will's mouth.

Holding hands, they stroll back to their suite. Patrick's legs shake slightly. "Room service," he grunts. He doesn't want to risk being strong armed into dining with Will's parents. So what if they don't make it to one of the extravagant luaus hosted on the resort. It's a small price to pay for avoiding more drama.

"Definitely," Will agrees. "Then let's read."

Patrick nods sharply. "Vampires, here I come."

It wouldn't be his life, though, if they made it back to their room without another brush with the unholy trinity.

"Will!" Kimberly calls out as they walk past the pool. She's in a lounger next to Angelica, her cheeks flushed from sun and God-only-knows what else. Angelica's tits are on display in a barely there bikini, and there are red marks on her neck. She waves excitedly at them. "Will come over here. I want to talk with you."

Will shakes his head and grips Patrick's arm, tugging him hard toward the building. "And, just like that, I'm tense again."

"Your mother has that effect on people."

"I wonder where my father is?"

"Let's hope we don't find out."

Once the door to their room is shut and locked behind them, Will falls onto the sofa in a heap. "Order a bunch of food," he says, eyes hooded with exhaustion. "I'm going to nap."

Patrick checks the reading on Will's monitor but doesn't argue. It's been a long, hot, sexy day, and he's tired too. Once they've both had fatty food and a nap, the world will be a brighter place.

"Yes, I'd like to put in an order for three hamburgers, two orders of onion rings, and a side of wings. Of course I want ranch dressing for the wings. Who wouldn't?" He carries on with their order, his eyes glued to Will's slack face.

Even in sleep Will makes his heart do silly things. Patrick loves the sensation though he wonders at himself that he's willing to risk feeling it for yet another creature. Once he's willingly squandered more of his heart and life to whatever child comes to them, he'll probably watch it sleep too. It's one of those inexplicably weird things about love he's grateful he's had the chance to learn.

Chapter Fourteen

"D R. MCCLOUD, JUST the man I've been looking for."

Patrick rolls his eyes. "All I wanted was to bang a hot guy in Vegas. That's all I wanted." He turns to a family walking past, saying to the children as their mother ushers them toward the pool, "Consequences are real, kids. Don't drink and hook up."

The woman shoots him a concerned glance and herds the children on more quickly just as Tony catches up to Patrick on the walkway.

Patrick shakes the bag in his hand, rattling the frozen Snickers bars he just picked up at the on-site convenience store. "Make it fast. I don't want Will's snack to melt."

Tony's smile dimples both cheeks, and Patrick rolls his eyes as his dick traitorously notices yet again how darkly handsome Will's father is. He wishes he could honestly say he doesn't know what Kimberly sees in the man, but the way sex oozes off him—all that dark glossy hair, those white teeth, and his hazel eyes—makes it hard to miss.

"You and I have unfinished business."

"Nope," Patrick says, turning his back on Tony. "I told you at Christmas and again the last time you were in Healing schtupping Kimberly, I'm not interested in a life of crime. Thanks. Bye."

Tony chuckles. "No, not about that. Not this time. I'm talking about the situation with Will."

Patrick lets out a sharp sigh. "What situation with Will? He's happy, healthy, and less insane than all of the rest of you put together. What more do you want?" He remembers past threats and clenches his hands together protectively. "And leave any mention of my fingers out of this."

Tony squeezes Patrick's shoulder warmly. "I'd never dream of doing any damage to those talent fingers. Not so long as my son *is*, as you say, happy, healthy, and…sober. *Is* he sober?"

"Yes."

"You're certain?"

"Aren't you?" Patrick shoots back. "You've got your goons hanging around Healing again. They'd have noticed if Will was hitting up the bars. Especially since that's how they spend their own evenings I'm sure. When they're not indulging at the whorehouse."

"Escort service," Tony corrects.

"Whatever."

Another family hustles by them, the father putting his hands over his daughter's ears and glaring at them. Obviously, this isn't a conversation fit for public consumption, but so few of his conversations are: either no one wants to hear about brains because of the gore factor or no one wants to hear about sex because of the TMI factor. In Patrick's opinion, that's their problem, not his.

"Rumor has it Will's ex has taken a turn for the worse and that my son is footing the bill for it."

"No, I'm footing the bill." Patrick rubs the bridge of his nose. It's tender still from the prior day's burn. Luckily, it doesn't seem bad enough to peel, but their honeymoon isn't over yet.

"And why would you do something like that?" Tony cocks his head, genuine curiosity shining in his eyes.

"I don't have to explain myself to you."

"No, I suppose you don't." Tony frowns. "I don't like the idea of that man—a man who hurt my son—"

"No small thanks to you."

"—getting a king's treatment."

"You'd rather he suffered?"

"Wouldn't you?" Tony says slyly, slipping an arm around Patrick's shoulders. "Payback for all he did to Will. All the pain and hurt he caused him?"

"No. I'm not a sociopath." Patrick shrugs him off. "So, let me get this straight. You came out tonight, leaving Kimberly and your bouncing bride alone, to give me the third degree about Ryan Whitehead's medical care? I call bull crap on that."

Tony shrugs. "I was going to the convenience store to buy more condoms actually. It's been a wild couple of days. But, when I spotted you without Will, I decided to investigate a few things I've been meaning to address with you alone. The other being Will's relationship with his mother."

"Talk to Will. That's between him and Kimber—" Patrick puts up his hand. "Never mind. Don't talk to him. You've interfered in our honeymoon enough."

"It's not as bad as you make it out to be. You've had plenty of time alone. I know because I've been so busy myself that I almost can't walk straight."

"This conversation is done."

"Not so fast."

Patrick glares at him before turning away. "Yes, so fast. You have nothing to say that interests me."

"You and Will should have dinner with us tomorrow night."

"Nope."

Tony smiles winningly. "It would go a long way toward soothing Kimberly's hurt feelings."

"Kimberly's hurt feel—" Patrick wipes a hand over his face. "You know what? Forget it. Go back to your little swingers party for three and leave me and your son alone."

It's only as Patrick's stalking away that it occurs to him that it's probably not wise to talk to a murdering mobster that way. But he shrugs and doesn't even look back over his shoulder. Because if there's one thing he's sure of about Tony Molinaro it's that he loves banging Kimberly Patterson.

And if there's one thing he's sure of about Kimberly Patterson, it's that she is obsessed in her own sick way with Will. That means Patrick's safe from the Molinaros and murder so long as Will is happy with him, and so long as Kimberly doesn't decide Patrick needs to be offed.

Probably.

It doesn't really matter. He'll take his chances rather than live in fear. Besides, Tony Molinaro seems to like it when Patrick puts him in his place. Maybe because no one else does.

Will sits in bed reading when Patrick comes back from his little surprise tête-à-tête with Tony with the bag of half-melted frozen Snickers bars. Patrick tosses the bag on the night table and opens his mouth to propose they play a kinky game with the candy, because apparently Hawaii's fresh, ocean air gives his dick teenage boy stamina again.

He stops in his tracks. Rivulets run down Will's face and he's red from the middle of his chest up, like he's been crying for a while now.

"What's wrong?" Patrick rushes to him, slips his hands into Will's hair, and lifts his head. "What's happened?"

"I hate this book!" Will exclaims, throwing the thick novel on the floor, his lips trembling. "I hate it so much!"

Will's willingness to express his feelings is something Patrick admires, though he sometimes finds it confusing as hell. He's been enjoying his vampire book, but even when he hates something he's reading, he doesn't cry about it. Taking a deep breath, he rolls with it. "I take it *A Little Life* is not the next great gay novel then?"

"It's so sad." Will's mouth crumples, and he leans over, crying into his hands. "It's so horribly sad."

Patrick's not big into literature, preferring to spend his too-few entertainment hours being actually *entertained*, but he's been through college. He's read *The City and the Pillar* and he's seen too many miserable gay films. He knows the score. "Aren't all 'great gay stories' sad?"

"No!"

Patrick considers. "I mean, someone has to die or commit suicide or there's no big important life lesson in it, right?"

"Stop."

Patrick awkwardly pats his back. "Want to tell me?" He kind of hopes Will doesn't, actually, but he'll listen if it'll make Will feel better. He suspects whatever he says in reply won't help much, though.

"It's too sad to talk about."

"Okay." Relief flows. He can just hold Will and that'll make it better in its own way. At least it usually does.

But as soon as Will's safe in his arms, tucked up against Patrick's chest in a reverse of their usual sleeping position, Will starts talking about the book again. He outlines the plot and says, "That's when I flipped ahead because it had to get better, right? *Right?*" He clutches

Patrick. "It didn't get better. It got worse."

"Sounds like a bad book."

"It's so unbelievable in one way, but in others…in the abuse and the way a young person can be led into doing things they never wanted to do." He swallows thickly, rubbing his cheek against Patrick's shirt. "It made me think about you and that man who—" His voice chokes. Patrick shudders. He prefers to forget. "And it reminded me of what happened between me and Ryan. And it made me think of other people too."

Patrick says nothing, stroking down Will's back. Life's plenty hard and maybe bringing a child into it is selfish and stupid. But he can't help thinking that he and Will are going to pull it off somehow. Maybe love has made him optimistic? He hopes not.

"Why is it so easy to break someone, Patrick? How can it be so simple to take a person and destroy them?"

Patrick has a feeling this is a rhetorical question. He's getting better at figuring those out. He used to just answer any question Will posed to him, willy-nilly, but time has proven that sometimes Will doesn't actually want answers. Especially not Patrick's answers. He kisses the top of Will's head instead.

"Abuse can happen to anyone." Will's voice is rough and haunted. "Even someone proud and strong. Someone like Hartley."

"Ah."

Of course Will hasn't forgotten about Ryan and Hartley. Caitlin telling him about Ryan is bound to bring up all kinds of memories and feelings, and being on their honeymoon isn't going to squash that completely. So, of course the abuse he's read about in the book forced it all to the surface again.

"I'm sorry," Will whispers. "I shouldn't be upset about Ryan. He was awful to me and—"

"It's fine." Patrick touches his cheek.

"Is it?"

"Yes." He clears his throat. "Besides, I read in *Bride Magazine*'s online special honeymoon edition that brides usually cry on their honeymoon. It's a thing."

"I'm not the bride," Will says, laughing wetly, poking Patrick's stomach. "You're the bride."

"We can both be the bride." He rubs Will's shoulder. "If lesbians can do it, so can we."

Will clasps him close. "Patrick?"

"Hmm?"

"Shut up."

They kiss for a long time and hold each other, their passion slowly growing, and eventually they fuck again. This time with the toy inserted so Patrick can pound the grief out of Will without hurting him. When it's over, they hold each other and Will cries some more. Patrick lets him, because it's the only thing he can do. No amount of logic is going to make Will not care about the dickwad who abused him for years. He's tried that before. It doesn't work.

Love is weird like that. He should know. He's going to have a baby with Will and bring it into the craziest family ever. Maybe Child Protection Services should intervene before they even get started.

After they've eaten the melted remains of the frozen Snickers bars in the middle of their wrecked sheets. Flushed from his recent tears and even more recent orgasm, Will's quiet for such a long time that a shiver passes over Patrick's sweaty skin. "You okay?" he asks eventually.

"With you? Yes." Will sighs. "With my past? No. I still can't believe the Ryan I loved became the Ryan who's dying."

"I know."

"Why does it hurt? I love you now. I don't even love him anymore, do I? Why does it hurt to think of him dying and Hartley so destroyed but loyal to him? Maybe I should have gone to see him."

"Do you want to go now?" Patrick smooths Will's hair off his forehead.

"No. I don't really want to see him ever again. I just never thought the way we ended it would really be the way we left it forever."

"You could call."

"You don't really want me to do that."

"No, but if it helps."

Will shakes his head. "Sometimes things are messy in life. Not everything is tied up with a bow and sealed with smiles and forgiveness."

"True."

Will's eyes go sad and distant again. "All of this

makes me wonder if it really is a good idea to bring another person into this world or into our lives."

Patrick purses his lips but eventually says, "I'd be lying if I said I wasn't having some of the same reservations."

"If we adopted, we'd just be taking care of a child already in the world. Not bringing one into our mess." Will gazes at him hopefully.

"But when I think of our child, I think of them looking like you," Patrick confesses.

"And I think of them looking like *you*."

Patrick laughs. "No. I've got alcoholism in my family and autism spectrum disorder and my skin burns in the sun. It should be you."

"I'm an alcoholic with Type 1 diabetes and my whole family is insane. It should be you."

"Maybe adoption," Patrick concedes.

"Or maybe we stir our sperm up in a petri dish and let fate decide."

"Sounds fun." Patrick clears his throat. "Speaking of fun, I ran into your dad. He wants us to have dinner with them tomorrow night."

"No. Absolutely not."

"Good. We're on the same page."

Will pulls Patrick close and breathes all sweet and chocolaty in his ear. "I want to leave for Kauai tomorrow morning before dawn. I know that wasn't the plan, and I know I said I wanted to stay here, but my parents are obviously bent on making me crazy."

"I agree." Patrick nuzzles him gently. He loves the

way Will smells after sex—earthy and all his. "And let me tell you the next honeymoon we go on will be very different. It'll be to Antarctica for the winter. No planes in or out. Just a lot of scientists I can geek out with and cute penguins for you to watch, puddin'-pop."

"Sounds perfect."

"It's a plan."

Will laughs and rolls his eyes, the sadness of earlier mostly dispelled. Patrick resolves to trash Will's miserable book before morning too. If he needs something to read, he can check out Patrick's awesome vampire book. Jenny was right. It is hot as hell and utterly ridiculous. It even has a gay vampire in it. It's the perfect vacation read.

As honeymoons go, Patrick knows this one hasn't been the most romantic in all of history, despite his planning and best efforts. Still, he wouldn't want to be on a honeymoon with anyone else in the entire world. He's only into this marriage thing at all because of his horrifyingly intense love for Will.

Patrick guesses he's satisfied. It actually could have been worse. He doesn't want to risk imagining just how, but he knows it could have been worse. At least they've had days of fucking and relaxing mixed in with the stress of Will's parents' mess. One day they'll laugh about it. Probably.

Will kisses him and snuggles closer. Patrick falls asleep with a smile on his face and a warm sense of contentment sliding over him.

Yes, it could have been so much worse.

Chapter Fifteen

THEY SNEAK OUT of the resort in the morning, return the rented Porsche, and charter a private jet to Kauai as the sun rises over the horizon. Will's sorry to say goodbye to the Big Island with so much still not checked off their to-do list, but Patrick just shrugs as they wait for the hired pilot to board their plane.

"It's not like we can't come back. We'll want to escape the kiddo once we have her."

"A girl?"

"Probably. Your sperm will make girls," Patrick says, pulling a small bag of chips and a bottle of water out of his briefcase. He throws back an anti-anxiety pill and chases it down with a chip.

"What? That's absurd."

"Sugar and spice and everything nice. Your sperm will make a girl. Trust me. Mine will make a really angry little boy."

"I can't believe you're a doctor sometimes."

"Doctors are allowed to believe illogical things too. It's a genius's prerogative."

Will rolls his eyes, but clicks his seat belt together

without arguing that Patrick's sperm is the more rational choice, or that Patrick never lets him believe illogical things just for the hell of it. They have time to debate it all later.

"Sorry for the delay," the short, smiling pilot says as he climbs aboard, with his dark hair wind-tousled and his eyes glittering happily. "We'll be on our way shortly."

The flight is uneventful but beautiful. Will can't keep his eyes off the play of colors on the water as the sun rises higher in the sky. Patrick falls asleep and snores adorably with his head on Will's shoulder.

Once they land, they rent a car and drive to the north side of the island. While they wait for their room to be prepared, they sip freshly squeezed juice on the new, posh hotel's veranda.

"We're free!" Patrick says, lifting his glass to toast the view.

"Knock on wood," Will insists. "Don't jinx it."

"We need to maximize the time we have left. What do you most want to do here?"

"Not much. I want to see a few sites, walk the hotel's strip of beach, eat good meals, and just be quiet with you."

"That seems easy enough."

"I'm easy to please, really."

"I've discovered that over the years. You should demand more."

Will just shrugs and they finish their juices while listening to morning bird song.

Finally ensconced in their beautifully appointed room, they nap for a few hours, holding each other in the cool sheets. When they wake in the early afternoon, they text Jenny to make sure she knows where they are in the event of a true emergency, and swear her to absolute secrecy on their whereabouts.

"Now, what do you want to do next, puddin'-pop?"

What follows are three days of easy joy. No drama tugs them under. No unwanted guests appear. They drift and read, chat and laugh, swim and explore the north side of the island. They discuss babies and how to make them. And they make love every day. They sleep deeply and well every night.

It's everything Will has ever wanted from a honeymoon and more.

At the end of their final day on Kauai, they settle at a table in the hotel's beautiful open-air bar to sip sodas, watch the sunset, and confront the reality that their trip is at an end. The bar is nearly empty, save for another couple eating dinner and talking quietly, a few servers, and the bartender. Everyone appears sun-soaked and dreamy in the early evening light.

Will alternates his gaze between the place where the sun slips lower and Patrick's auburn hair glittering red and blond in the dying light. Their silence is peaceful. The light music playing overhead, the calls of birds, and the gentle hum of the hotel bar employees' conversations buoys Will's spirits even higher.

"No use putting it off," Patrick says finally, pulling

his cell phone out of the back pocket of his white shorts. "Are you ready?"

Will shakes his head, unwilling to pop the beautiful bubble they've been living in quite yet. "Just a few more minutes. And then we can do it."

Patrick places the phone on the table in front of them and dutifully waits.

Eventually, after the sun has been swallowed by the sea, and they've both had two more sodas, Will pulls his phone out and gives Patrick the go-ahead. He shudders as their phones ping with dozens of texts.

Will glimpses incoming messages from Owen, Kevin, Caitlin, and one from Olivia, plus a bunch from his mom and a few from his dad before they're swallowed by Good Works-related texts and old weather alerts.

"I don't know where to start." Will chooses to open the one from Olivia first, in case his youngest sister needs him.

Connor stole my Army boots and wore them into the creek on the farm. They got stuck in the mud and he left them there. Now I can't find them and even if I could they're probably ruined. I hate him.

Okay, not great, but not an emergency. It can wait. He scrolls to the message from Caitlin next.

Patrick interrupts him before he can read it. "Good news. Jenny says she's kicked Tom to the curb."

"And Jax?"

"Begged him to forgive her."

"Did he take her back?"

"Looks like."

"Tell her not to mess it up again," Will says, skimming Caitlin's message about school, her dorm, and her decision to rush a sorority.

Patrick nods and types in his reply. "That's it. The hospital actually respected my order not to text me, shocking as that is. There are texts from your mom that basically accuse us of ruining her trip by leaving without discussing it with her first. Won't dignify those with a response. And I'm done. I won't risk further exposure to the outside world." He powers down his phone.

Will replies to Caitlin and offers to cover the expense of anything she's forgotten to take or anything she needs.

"Like birth control," Patrick quips, reading over his shoulder.

Will frowns. But then adds a line about birth control and his willingness to pay for the pills if need be. He gathers from the texts from Kevin that his mother still hasn't returned from her jaunt to meet up with his father, but nothing in Kevin's messages seems urgent.

He texts his uncle anyway with their anticipated arrival time the next day. He ignores the Good Works texts, because surely Owen has everything under control. And, if he doesn't, then Will can wait until he's back in Healing to deal with it all.

Then, through half-squinted eyes, he opens the string of texts from his mother, dating all the way back to before she crashed their honeymoon. Quickly, he messages her that they're leaving Hawaii tomorrow, and he'll see her back home in Healing. "That should do it."

"Quick, shut down before she can reply," Patrick urges him.

But before he can, his phone pings with a message from Uncle Kevin.

I hate to be the bearer of bad news, but you should know that Ryan passed away last night.

Will's mouth goes dry, cold chills race over him, and a lump fills his throat. The world around him whistles in a wind tunnel of shock.

Patrick grabs his phone out of his hands, and Will realizes he's been staring at the message, unresponsive, for a long time. After a minute, Patrick powers down the phone and takes hold of Will's hand. "Let's get out of here."

Will nods.

Out of the corner of his eye, Will sees Patrick motioning for a server. "Charge it to the room." Then he grips Will by his arm and gently hauls him to a standing position. "C'mon, puddin'-pop." His voice is sandpaper rough. "Let's take a walk to the beach."

Will stumbles several times on the trail surrounded by flowering bushes leading down to the empty, sandy beach, still strewn with footsteps of earlier beach goers.

Everyone seems to have retreated to their rooms or the hotel restaurant for the evening, and Will's grateful for it. He'd hate for a bunch of strangers to see him cry, and the idea of going to their room, spacious and beautiful as it is, feels too claustrophobic to hold all of his emotions.

Because he's having big ones.

Emotions that don't even feel like they fit inside his body. They crash out all around him like water on the rocks and beat at the seams of him like the waves on the sand. The ocean breathes his pain, holds it, and then smashes it out again.

"It shouldn't hurt like this," he says finally. "It shouldn't even matter."

"Don't be ridiculous." Patrick pulls him down to sit on the sand near a shady outcropping of rocks. "Of course it matters. You loved him. He was a big part of your life, for better or worse, and you're too good of a person to want this to be how it ended for him."

"I wanted him to be happy. That's all I ever wanted for him. It's why I let him treat me the way he did. I never wanted him to die miserable." He wiped the tears from his cheeks. "And I hate that he died still hurting someone else."

Patrick rubs Will's back, his hand soothing and famil-iar. "Should we text for information on the funeral?"

"No." Will shakes his head, tears rolling off his chin and splashing, hot and surprising, against his exposed knees. He kicks off his flip-flops and digs his toes into the rough, yellow sand.

He stares out at the rolling water, grateful that Pat-rick doesn't say anything. His hand on Will's back is the exact weight that he needs to hold him together.

"I really want a drink," Will says. "More than I've wanted one in a long time."

Patrick still says nothing. He just strokes Will's back slowly. They sit together watching the moon rise above the horizon.

Will closes his eyes, and more tears slip down his face. Wordlessly, he leans against Patrick, finally giving into sobs, and folds down to pillow his head on Patrick's thigh. Patrick runs his fingers through his hair. The moon continues to rise.

Eventually, Will's tears stop, and he wipes his eyes with the edge of Patrick's shirt. "I'm ready," he whispers, rising to his feet and reaching down to help Patrick up. "It's been long past time to say goodbye to Ryan."

Patrick remains quiet, and they walk hand-in-hand to their room, where they shower before climbing into bed to curl in each other's arms.

"I want to help Hartley," Will says, nuzzling Patrick's soft hair.

"If he'll accept your help, that's fine by me."

"And if he doesn't?"

"There isn't much you can do. He's been through a lot."

"Yeah." Will swallows hard and squeezes Patrick closer. "I owe you so much for opening my eyes to what real love feels like."

"Ditto."

Will smiles, his heart aching with bittersweet feelings.

"Hartley deserves to know real love too."

"You planning to show him?"

"No."

"Then there's not much you can do about that either. Let Hartley find his own way. He's strong."

"He's been broken."

Patrick kisses Will's chest and rubs his cheek against his chest hair. "No, he's strong. That was Ryan's type, you know. The stronger, the better. The more fun to break."

Will remembers the prideful Hartley he once knew and has to admit Patrick's on to something. "I still want to be there for him."

"Fine. But when he bites your head off, don't say I didn't warn you."

"Can you make me forget?"

Patrick trails a hand down to Will's crotch. "Like this?"

"No," Will murmurs, tugging Patrick's mouth up for a kiss. "Like this."

They kiss sweetly for a long time. Eventually, mouths raw and sore, they rub against each other until they come. It's enough to leave Will sleepy and ready to let go for the night.

Patrick cleans them up, checks Will's monitor, and then assumes his sleeping position: head on Will's chest, arm slung across his stomach. It's familiar and comforting. It's right.

"Sleep tight, puddin'-pop," Patrick slurs as he drifts

off.

Will stares at the moon outside their hotel room window. It shines on the waves, illuminating the comfortable darkness of their room. The next morning they'll fly home and life will start up where it left off. There'll be family to cope with, jobs to do, and, in Patrick's case, patients and nurses to cure and offend. They'll have life to live, and a future life to plan.

Tears swim up to the surface again as he realizes that it's all so precious, and so perfect, and all squandered by the man he'd first given his heart away to years ago.

Squandered and lost for good. How horrible, how meaningless, how sad.

"Sleep," Patrick whispers. "It'll all still be there to-morrow."

Obediently, Will closes his eyes. It doesn't take long at all for dreams to catch him. Thankfully, sleep steals his grief away.

THE NEXT MORNING, Patrick knows Will's still hurting, but his shoulders are back and his chin is up as they wait at the airport for their pilot to arrive so they can take the Good Works jet home.

"Well, this hasn't been the honeymoon I expected but I can't say I was bored," Patrick offers, putting out his hand.

Will grips it tightly and smiles. The light Patrick usually finds in his eyes is duller than usual, but not entirely missing. "Me either."

"I turned my phone on this morning while you were still sleeping," Patrick confesses. "Made a few calls. Paid a few bills."

"Ryan's funeral services."

He nods.

Will's lips tremble, but he swallows hard, getting a visible grip on his emotions. "I love you. And you didn't have to do that."

"He's part of you, for better or worse."

"But we shouldn't clean up Ryan's mistakes. I did that for a long time. Took the blame and the brunt of it all." Patrick watches as Will's eyes open wider. He's getting it now. "This isn't about Ryan. It's about Hartley."

Patrick shrugs. "Why should he worry about how to afford a funeral when he's probably confused about how to carry on with his life now? It's no skin off my nose to take care of everything."

"You're such a secret softy."

Patrick frowns. "Not according to Ruby Lovell. She's been fired and her license revoked." He narrows his eyes and crosses his arms. "Good riddance."

The pilot joins them on the tarmac, and they board the Good Works jet shortly thereafter. Will takes his usual seat by the window, and Patrick downs his anti-anxiety meds with a half a turkey sandwich the pilot has for him in the cooler.

"Thank you," Will says quietly as Patrick's nodding off. "For this honeymoon. For marrying me in Vegas. For sticking with me through everything."

Patrick rouses himself enough to reply, "Don't be an idiot. I'm the one who should thank you. Now let me sleep."

Will's lips are soft on Patrick's forehead, and Patrick slips into sleep not long after the plane hits cruising altitude. His dreams are full of brains and victory, and he wakes when they land to refuel in Los Angeles with anticipation flooding his system.

Hours and hours later, he's finally home again. Their house in Healing is a welcome sight after the endless tin can of an airplane and the drive from the airport. It's after midnight, but they're both still wide awake, stuck back on Hawaii time and overly rested from the naps on the plane.

"Well, we're here," Will says, dropping his luggage on the kitchen floor and stretching his arms wide. He's a disheveled mess, with wild hair, and his shorts and shirt wrinkled from the travel. "Home sweet home."

Patrick takes a deep breath. The maid has been by and the kitchen smells like lavender cleanser and lemons, and he loves it. "Ten days away with no social media. I'm gonna pop some corn and log in to *The Hurting Times* ASAP." He rubs his hands together. "See what I've been missing."

Will laughs and slings his lightest bag over his shoulder. "Do that. I'm going to download some of the photos from my camera to my laptop so I can text them to Dinah like she asked."

"That was the one bummer about not having our phones, wasn't it?" Patrick mutters, grabbing a bowl for the popcorn and kicking the rest of their luggage out of the way. They can deal with unpacking later.

"I didn't mind carrying the camera. Though I guess we took a lot fewer pictures than we normally would have."

"Good thing I'm a genius with a photographic memory."

"So you claim."

It's easy how quickly they fall back into old habits, though everything feels mildly surreal given the late hour. After they're both comfortable on the sofa with their respective screens, Patrick grabs handfuls of popcorn and shoves it into his mouth as he skims through ten days worth of Healing's gossip.

"Oh, ho, listen to this about Jenny." He nudges Will with his shoulder. "This is from when she kicked out Tom: *Our favorite blonde heartbreaker is breaking hearts again. This time she's kicking baby-daddy to the curb despite his promises to stick around. Rumor has it, she's missing all that hot coffee lovin' from our favorite barista now that she's been reminded of the sadly uninspiring length of baby-daddy's D.*" Patrick laughs until there are tears in his eyes.

"Guess you'll be calling Jenny first thing in the morning."

"Of course. Need to know all about her baby-daddy's D." He snorts and wipes at his eyes. "Holy cripes, have I ever told you how much I love it here?"

"What?" Laughing, Will sets aside his laptop. "Seriously? Are you still high from those anti-anxiety meds?"

"They don't make me high. Just relaxed. And maybe, but I do love it here. It's the absolute trashiest, most drama-riddled town of all time, and I love it. Not as much as I love you, but…" He cracks up again, his face growing splotchy with laughter. "It's so awful it follows us halfway around the world."

"So you're content to raise a kid here?" Will asks once Patrick's calmed down.

"Sure. Speaking of, let's try to make one for ourselves one last time." He waggles his eyebrows. "Maybe we just haven't tried hard enough."

Will flushes, his eyes shining. "Pretty sure I don't have the right parts."

"You know what I always say: If at first you don't succeed, try, try again."

"I thought you always say that I'm a great lay."

"That too. C'mon, let's finish this the way it began." Patrick stands up and pulls Will along with him. "With you shouting my name."

As they walk up the stairs to the bedroom, Will whispers, "Want to play superhero and villain again?"

"No." Patrick kisses Will's cheek before whispering in his ear, "Let's just play Will and Patrick."

THE END

Letter from Leta

Dear Reader,

Thank you so much for reading *Will & Patrick Wake Up Married, Episode 7*! This story was a delight to write with my friend Alice Griffiths, and I hope that you enjoyed reading it as much as we enjoyed crafting it. Bonus scenes for *Will & Patrick*, as well as extra stories for other book universes, can be found at my Patreon.

Be sure to follow me on BookBub or Goodreads to be notified of new releases. And look for me on Facebook for snippets of the day-to-day writing life, or join my Facebook Group for announcements and special giveaways. To see some sources of my inspiration, you can follow my Pinterest boards or Instagram.

If you enjoyed the book, please take a moment to leave a review! Reviews not only help readers determine if a book is for them, but also help a book show up in site searches.

Also, for the audiobook connoisseurs out there, *Will & Patrick Wake Up Married, Episodes 1-6* is available narrated by the wonderfully talented John Solo. Many of my other books are also in audio, also narrated by John Solo or Michael Ferraiuolo. I hope to eventually add my entire backlist to my audiobook roster over the next few years.

Thank you for being a reader!
Leta

WILL & PATRICK'S ENDLESS HONEYMOON

by Leta Blake

In Healing, South Dakota, marriage is never boring!

Genius brain surgeon Patrick McCloud never thought he'd fall in love, let alone get married. He and Will Patterson are two years overdue for their honeymoon, and although romance doesn't come naturally to Patrick, he's determined to make it perfect.

Will works himself to the bone helping others and dealing with his family, who bring the drama nonstop. A tropical getaway without the usual shenanigans is just what the doctor ordered. But can Will's family leave them in peace? Knowing the Patterson-Molinaro clan, it's not likely…

Will and Patrick's Endless Honeymoon by Leta Blake continues the soapy, sexy fun of the original six part *Wake Up Married* serial. In Healing, South Dakota, marriage is never boring!

ANY GIVEN LIFETIME

by Leta Blake

He'll love him in any lifetime.

Neil isn't a ghost, but he feels like one. Reincarnated with all his memories from his prior life, he spent twenty years trapped in a child's body, wanting nothing more than to grow up and reclaim the love of his life.

As an adult, Neil finds there's more than lost time separating them. Joshua has built a beautiful life since Neil's death, and how exactly is Neil supposed to introduce himself? As Joshua's long-dead lover in a new body? Heartbroken and hopeless, Neil takes refuge in his work, developing microscopic robots called nanites that can produce medical miracles.

When Joshua meets a young scientist working on a medical project, his soul senses something his rational mind can't believe. Has Neil truly come back to him after twenty years? And if the impossible is real, can they be together at long last?

Any Given Lifetime is a stand-alone, slow burn, second chance gay romance by Leta Blake featuring reincarnation and true love. This story includes some angst, some steam, an age gap, and, of course, a happy ending.

VESPERTINE

by Leta Blake & Indra Vaughn

Can a priest and a rock star obey love's call?

Seventeen years ago, Jasper Hendricks and Nicholas Blumfeld's childhood friendship turned into a secret, blissful love affair. They spent several idyllic months together until Jasper's calling to the Catholic priesthood became impossible to ignore. Left floundering, Nicky followed his own trajectory into rock stardom, but he never stopped looking back.

Today, Jasper pushes boundaries as an out, gay priest, working hard to help vulnerable LGBTQ youth. He's determined to bring change to the church and the world. Respected, admired, and settled in his skin, Jasper has long ignored his loneliness.

As Nico Blue, guitarist and songwriter for the band Vespertine, Nicky owns the hearts of millions. He and his bandmates have toured the world, lighting their fans on fire with their music. Numbed by drugs and fueled by simmering anger, Nicky feels completely alone. When Vespertine is forced to get sober, Nicky returns home to where it all started.

Jasper and Nicky's careers have ruled their lives since they parted as teens. When they come face to face again, they must choose between the past's lingering ghosts or the promise of a new future.

THE RIVER LEITH

by Leta Blake

Amnesia stole his memories, but it can't erase their love.

Leith is terrified after waking up in a hospital bed to find his most recent memories are three years out of date.

Worse, he can't even remember how he met the beautiful man who visits him most days. Everyone claims Zach is his best friend, but Leith's feelings for Zach aren't friendly.

They're so much more than that.

Zach fills Leith with longing. Attraction. Affection. **Lust**. And those feelings are even scarier than losing his memory, because Leith's always been straight. Hasn't he?

For Zach, being forgotten by his lover is excruciating. Leith's amnesia has stolen everything: their relationship, their happiness, and the man he loves. Suddenly single and alone, Zach knows nothing will ever be okay again.

Desperate to feel better, Zach confesses his grief to the faceless Internet. But his honesty might come back to haunt them both.

The River Leith is a standalone MM romance with amnesia trope, hurt/comfort, bisexual discovery, "first time" gay scenes, a second chance at first love, and a satisfying happy ending.

Gay Romance Newsletter

Leta's newsletter will keep you up to date on her latest releases, sales and deals, future writing plans, and more from the world of M/M romance. Join Leta's mailing list today.

Leta Blake on Patreon

Become part of Leta Blake's Patreon community to support her indie publishing expenses and to access exclusive content, deleted scenes, extras, and interviews.

Other Books by Leta Blake

Contemporary

Will & Patrick Wake Up Married
Will & Patrick's Endless Honeymoon
Cowboy Seeks Husband
The Difference Between
Bring on Forever
Stay Lucky

Sports

The River Leith

The Training Season Series
Training Season
Training Complex

Musicians

Smoky Mountain Dreams
Vespertine

New Adult

Punching the V-Card

'90s Coming of Age Series
Pictures of You
You Are Not Me
Only You

Winter Holidays

North's Pole

The Mr. Christmas Series
Mr. Frosty Pants
Mr. Naughty List
Mr. Jingle Bells

A Boy for All Seasons
My December Daddy

Fantasy

Any Given Lifetime

Reimagined Fairy Tales

Flight
Levity

Paranormal & Shifters

Angel Undone
Omega Mine

Horror

Raise Up Heart

Omegaverse

Heat of Love Series
White Heat
Slow Heat
Alpha Heat
Slow Birth
Bitter Heat

For Sale Series
Heat for Sale
Bully for Sale

Audiobooks
letablake.com/audiobooks

Discover more about the author online

Leta Blake
letablake.com

About the Author

Author of the bestselling book *Smoky Mountain Dreams* and fan favorites like *Training Season*, *Will & Patrick Wake Up Married*, and *Slow Heat*, Leta Blake has been captivating M/M Romance readers for over a decade. Whether writing contemporary romance or fantasy, she puts her psychology background to use creating complex characters and love stories that feel real. At home in the Southern U.S., Leta works hard at achieving balance between her writing and her family life.